The Analog Sea Review

NUMBER TWO

THE ANALOG SEA REVIEW · NUMBER TWO

Copyright © 2019 Analog Sea

The acknowledgments on pp. 216–218 constitute
an extension of this copyright page.

Published by Analog Sea
PO Box 11670
Austin, Texas 78711
United States

Basler Strasse 115
79115 Freiburg
Germany

Editors Jonathan S. Simons
and Janos Tedeschi
Editorial Assistant Elena Fritz

Cover Artwork
Joseph-Antoine d'Ornano

ISBN 978-1-7322519-5-3

The Analog Sea Review
Number Two

Letter to the New Generation
Jonathan Simons

From the Editor

The new technologies, reaching now into every part of our lives, capturing so much of our attention, flooding our retinas constantly with artificial light, are making us passive. We're forgetting what sets us apart from animals and algorithms, what makes us more than half human.

True curiosity springs from deeper within us than shopping. It wants more than information and entertainment. Fleeing solitude does not enliven our creative faculties any more than an itch guided the brushstrokes of Michelangelo.

It's time we accept that the Internet failed, that it never became that heaven of absolute freedom we dreamed of. Such good intentions we had to create a country no church or parliament could fathom. Rising above the corporate, unidirectional media of our parents' generation, we became active cocreators, proudly constructing our libertarian paradise in the sky. Now the Internet calls us by name and mirrors our image constantly. After thirty years of unbridled enthusiasm, thirty years ensconced in digital's relentless sheen, it's time to accept that our global village bears little resemblance to that orchard of art and ideas we were hoping for.

In the Internet age, the gap between the question and the answer has dwindled to seconds. We once had no choice but to sit and wonder. Before the flickering blue screens came and eradicated boredom, we could not always evade that reluctant leaning into silence, emotions, and the void. In return, boredom gave us longing and ideas. Longing gave us empathy. And ideas gave us hope. New experiences were valuable because we could not access them anytime, anywhere. And anticipation, that buoyant tightrope stretched between wanting and having, made life thrilling. We had questions without answers. We had imagination.

In the Internet age, the algorithm tells us what we're looking for before we start looking. We see images of every place we go before arriving. There is no time for drifting or wandering, no time for staring up at the stars. What becomes of a child who has never found himself on the fringes of some wilderness, never lost, never lonely?

Long have we tried to escape the dull ache of boredom. The Greeks had their seventy-two-hour tragedies, and the Spanish their bloody bullfights. We invented religion, sports, and shopping malls. Television nearly anesthetized us, but we remained compelled to occasionally shut off the screen and return to our own lives. Before the cable operators snaked their way into our homes, back when over-the-air broadcast was our best option, each night ended with thirty minutes of local news and an anthem. The slow drip of spectacle then suddenly transformed into a wall of unpalatable static. The nights remained seedbeds of darkness and silence through which we slept and dreamed. Sometimes we felt alone. Now we look ever outward, at ephemera, at plates of glass, at our networks, at the images surrounding us on all sides, like prisoners with our faces pushed into the bars.

Boredom may have been uncomfortable, but it was a polestar we used to navigate the uncharted boundaries of thought and feeling. Boredom and solitude, two shores between which we taught ourselves how to swim.

And now you, the new generation, of course you don't want the world of your grandparents, a world of messy physicality, old age, limitations of all kinds, and boredom. In your new virtual world, everyone can pick up that big fat microphone and broadcast their own commercials across the globe. In your new virtual world, you don't have to worry about all those handshakes, all that awkward eye contact, all that skin and sweat, all those tears and runaway emotions. You don't have to worry about going blind from staring up at the sun all afternoon. In your new virtual world, you can have your fifteen minutes of fame all day long.

Now the marketplace is always on, and as soon as we reach out to grab that one digital fix—before we're able to post a comment or snap a photo—another cues up for our attention, *ad infinitum*. In the Internet age, we never catch up. We are perpetually lagging behind and haven't even the time to wonder how else to live our lives.

On Dreams
Lin Yutang

Discontent, they say, is divine; I am quite sure anyway that discontent is human. The monkey was the first morose animal, for I have never seen a truly sad face in animals except in the chimpanzee. And I have often thought such a one a philosopher, because sadness and thoughtfulness are so akin. There is something in such a face which tells me that he is thinking. Cows don't seem to think, at least they don't seem to philosophize, because they look always so contented, and while elephants may store up a terrific anger, the eternal swinging of their trunks seems to take the place of thinking and banish all brooding discontent. Only a monkey can look thoroughly bored with life. Great indeed is the monkey!

Perhaps after all, philosophy began with the sense of boredom. Anyway it is characteristic of humans to have a sad, vague and wistful longing for an ideal. Living in a real world, man has yet the capacity and tendency to dream of another world. Probably the difference between man and the monkeys is that the monkeys are merely bored, while man has boredom plus imagination. All of us have the desire to get out of an old rut, and all of us wish to be something else, and all of us dream. The private dreams of being a corporal, the corporal dreams of being a captain, and the captain dreams of being a major or colonel. A colonel, if he is worth his salt, thinks nothing of being a colonel. In more graceful phraseology, he calls it merely an opportunity to serve his fellow men. And really there is very little else to it. The plain fact is, Joan Crawford thinks less of Joan Crawford and Janet Gaynor than the world thinks of them. "Aren't you remarkable?" the world says to all the great, and the great, if they are truly great, always reply, "What is remarkable?" The world is therefore pretty much like an *à la carte* restaurant where everybody thinks the food the next table has ordered is so much more inviting and delicious than his own. A contemporary Chinese professor has made the witticism that in the matter of desirability, "Wives are always better if they are others', while writing is always better if it is one's own." In this sense, there is no one completely satisfied in this world. Everyone wants to be somebody so long as that somebody is not himself.

This human trait is undoubtedly due to our power of imagination and our capacity for dreaming. The greater the imaginative power of a man, the more perpetually he is dissatisfied. That is why an imaginative child is always a more difficult child; he is more often sad and morose like a monkey than happy and contented like a cow. Also divorce must necessarily be more common among the idealists and the more imaginative people than among the unimaginative. The vision of a desirable ideal life companion has an irresistible force which the less imaginative and less idealistic never feel. On the whole, humanity is as much led astray as led upwards by this capacity for idealism, but human progress without this imaginative gift is itself unthinkable.

Man, we are told, has aspirations. They are very laudable things to have, for aspirations are generally classified as noble. And why not? Whether as individuals or as nations, we all dream and act more or less in accordance with our dreams. Some dream a little more than others, as there is a child in every family who dreams more and perhaps one who dreams less. And I must confess to a secret partiality for the one who dreams. Generally he is the sadder one, but no matter; he is also capable of greater joys and thrills and heights of ecstasy. For I think we are constituted like a receiving set for ideas, as radio sets are equipped for receiving music from the air. Some sets with a finer response pick up the finer short waves which are lost to the other sets, and why, of course, that finer, more distant music is all the more precious if only because it is less easily perceivable.

And those dreams of our childhood, they are not so unreal as we might think. Somehow they stay with us throughout our life. That is why, if I had my choice of being any one author in the world, I would be Hans Christian Andersen rather than anybody else. To write the story of *The Mermaid*, or to be the Mermaid ourselves, thinking the Mermaid's thoughts and aspiring to be old enough to come up to the surface of the water, is to have felt one of the keenest and most beautiful delights that humanity is capable of.

And so, out in an alley, up in an attic, or down in the barn or lying along the waterside, a child always dreams, and the dreams are real. So Thomas Edison dreamed. So Robert Louis Stevenson dreamed. So Sir Walter Scott dreamed. All three dreamed in their childhood. And out of the stuff of such magic dreams are woven some of the finest and most beautiful fabrics we have ever seen. But these dreams are also partaken of by lesser children. The delights they get are as great, if the visions or contents of their dreams are different. Every child has a soul which yearns, and carries a longing on his lap and goes to sleep with it, hoping to find his dream come true when he wakes up with the morn. He tells no one of these dreams, for these dreams are his own, and for that reason they are a part of his innermost growing self. Some of these children's dreams are clearer than others, and they have a force which compels their own realization; on the other hand, with growing age, those less clear dreams are forgotten, and we all live through life trying to tell those dreams of our childhood, and "sometimes we die ere we find the language."

And so with nations, too. Nations have their dreams and the memories of such dreams persist through generations and centuries. Some of these are noble dreams, and others wicked and ignoble. The dreams of conquest and of being bigger and stronger than all the others are always bad dreams, and such nations always have more to worry about than others who have more peaceful dreams. But there are other and better dreams, dreams of a better world, dreams of peace and of nations living at peace with one another, and dreams of less cruelty, injustice, and poverty and suffering. The bad dreams tend to destroy the good dreams of humanity, and there is a struggle and a fight between these good and bad dreams. People fight for their dreams as much as they fight for their earthly possessions. And so dreams descend from the world of idle visions and enter the world of reality, and become a real force in our life. However vague they are, dreams have a way of concealing themselves and leave us no peace until they are translated into reality, like seeds germinating under ground, sure to sprout in their search for the sunlight. Dreams are very real things.

Lin Yutang, *The Importance of Living* (New York: Reynal & Hitchcock, 1937), pp. 73–76.

Is My Soul Asleep?
Antonio Machado

Is my soul asleep?
Have those beehives that labor
at night stopped? And the water
wheel of thought,
is it dry, the cups empty,
wheeling, carrying only shadows?

No my soul is not asleep.
It is awake, wide awake.
It neither sleeps nor dreams, but watches,
its clear eyes open,
far-off things, and listens
at the shores of the great silence.

Antonio Machado, *Times Alone: Selected Poems of Antonio Machado*, trans. Robert Bly (Middletown: Wesleyan University Press, 1983), p. 45.

Dream Poems
Robert Bly

Antonio Machado wrote some of his dream poems in his first book, *Soledades*, in 1899. Freud published his *Interpretation of Dreams* the same year. Machado independently makes dreams a primary subject of his poems, descends into them, looks to them for guidance, goes downward, farther and farther until he finds water. The water he has found makes *Soledades* refreshing.

One could say that "the world" exerts tremendous pressure on the psyche; collective opinion terrorizes the soul; the demands of the world obsess the psyche, and the world and its attractions offer to use up all the time available. Each person needs then, early on, to go inside, far enough inside to water the plants, awaken the animals, become friends with the desires, and sense what Machado calls "the living pulse of the spirit,"[1] start the fire in the hearth, and close the door so that what is inside us has sufficient power to hold its own against the forces longing to invade.

Machado has achieved this inner strengthening by the time he finishes his first book, and his praise of dreams is clear. His confidence rises from some source far below the intellect, far below even the security provided by the

---

1 Originally, "Honda palpitación del espíritu," in Antonio Machado, *Soledades* (Madrid: A. Alvarez, 1903).—*Ed.*

healthy mind in the healthy body. This sort of confidence seems to spring from earliest infancy. The positive, energetic mother holds the child near her heart, and he looks out on the world: it seems all blossoming, all good, and he carries that confidence with him all his life.

The Westerner, after centuries of extroverted science, and determined philosophical attempts to remove soul from conversation, architecture, observation, and education, sees inside himself, and sees what the ancients saw, but can hardly believe it.

Excerpted from an introduction by translator Robert Bly to *Times Alone: Selected Poems of Antonio Machado* (Middletown: Wesleyan University Press, 1983), pp. 11–12.

Dream Game
William Oxley

I see back down the years without sadness
and what I see is everybody's place,
a dark valley and a womb full of starlight.

Then life begins with the first short light
that grows longer, hours longer
until whole days form like huge mirrors

and we begin to play the dream game.
The dream game of life. And it's great
and beautiful to play this game and

watch everyone else also playing it. Exciting,
revelatory as for children moving nursery
toys, singing. Some would say it's chess,

or like chess, formalized as any business
with rules to chew on. But it's more than
this, it's wonderful, divine almost. Divine

as the love everyone is working towards,
and getting there until the mistakes begin.
Mistakes that let death and sadness, even money in.

The Pursuit of Wonder
Geoff Pevere

Peter Mettler admits to a lifelong captivation with the pursuit of wonder. He makes films that are part of an ongoing journey toward a heightened consciousness. His films shift shapes, textures and forms constantly, and there is not a single Mettler film that doesn't call upon a form of hyphenated categorization, as though he is always searching for the most appropriate means of expressing the inexpressible.

When he uses his own voiceover, as he does in *Picture of Light,* it's frequently to pose questions about the practical challenge of recording the unseen. For Mettler, the camera is not a medium for capturing reality but a means of seeing beyond it.

Geoff Pevere, "Peter Mettler: The Pursuit of Wonder," *Take One Magazine* (September–November 2004), p. 35–39.

Picture of Light
Peter Mettler

At the beginning of life there was only the real thing. Now there is media that records, regurgitates, preserves, dictates, and expresses. We know what is by what is represented, as much as by what we have seen for ourselves. We live in a time where things do not seem to exist unless they are contained as an image. But if you look into this darkness, you may see the lights of your own retina. Not unlike the northern lights. Not unlike the movements of thought. Like a shapeless accumulation of everything we've ever seen.

These images and sounds are articulations of experience. We look at them and try to decipher the reality that gave birth to them. It may well be that the northern lights cannot be filmed, that nature cannot be filmed, that film or media is in conflict with nature. Is it just a surrogate for the real thing? Is film a surrogate for real experience?

Soon we'll be able to stand in a virtual world, one that we've created with wires and pulses. It will entertain us. It will keep us busy.

Narration excerpted from *Picture of Light*, directed by Peter Mettler (Toronto, Canada: Grimthorpe Film, 1994), 35 mm, 83 minutes.

Interview with Peter Mettler
Janos Tedeschi

S wiss-Canadian filmmaker Peter Mettler is a singular
figure in contemporary cinema, a visionary explorer of
the intermediate worlds of our perception, a poet in search of
wonder. Mettler's films are meditations on our relationships
with the invisible, with nature and technology, and with
the medium of film itself. Mesmerized by *Picture of Light*,[1]
Mettler's extraordinary attempt to capture the aurora borealis
on celluloid, *Analog Sea Review* editors Jonathan Simons
and Janos Tedeschi traveled deep into the rural Appenzell
region of Switzerland for an afternoon of conversation with
the filmmaker. Here Mettler lives in a snug wooden chalet
surrounded by rolling hills and the silence of nature.

JANOS TEDESCHI: Have we now arrived in the virtual
world you predicted twenty-five years ago in your film
Picture of Light?

PETER METTLER: We're getting closer and closer. I wrote
that in '94 and it was still, for us, analog days. We were shooting on celluloid film and there was television and radio and
all that. I don't even think we were using the Internet yet

---

1 *Picture of Light*, directed by Peter Mettler (Toronto, Canada: Grimthorpe
Film, 1994), 35 mm, 83 minutes. Filmed in Churchill, Manitoba, Canada.

when we made that film. We actually shipped exposed film back to the city which was processed and returned to us to watch on an old 16 mm projector in a motel room days later.

That experience of filming the northern lights—we went to make a film without knowing what the thesis was. The objective was primarily to get the northern lights on film, and I was keeping a diary and developing feelings and ideas and themes over the course of making the film. But the thing that struck me so intensely was standing outside at minus thirty degrees Celsius in the middle of the night, watching these incredible dances of light, and realizing that no film was ever going to give anybody that experience. And there I was making a film. Why? In some ways to say, "Look how great the northern lights are." But ultimately the film became a question about what our relationship is to the real world and how much we trust the images. Are we even aware that our makeup, our consciousness, is so informed by mediated images that we don't really know things from the real world? So that's how it went.

JONATHAN SIMONS: There's a big difference between how one experiences, let's say, a patch of trees, versus the word *tree,* versus a photograph of a tree, versus a video of a tree. These questions interest me a lot, but especially now talking to you. Because it seems clear to me that you've been thinking about this relationship between representation and direct experience for a long time.

PM: The irony is that making films, using cameras, actually does make me see more deeply into things. But it also makes me see more deeply into the paradox that we learn about ourselves by documenting ourselves; by making images of ourselves all the time, we're learning about our identity. It's like taking poison, if you want to be extreme about it: the poison of the technology of the image you're making. And you're using it like homeopathy to understand better what it's doing to you and how you can then move forward, how you can integrate it. I think that relates to a lot of technology these days.

JS: Wim Wenders[2] was quite involved with still photography until a number of years ago, when he said he just couldn't bring himself to take pictures anymore because they're everywhere. Everyone's taking pictures.

PM: Wim Wenders is about fifteen years older than I am, but even when I went to film school, it was a geeky thing to do. There were not that many people applying. It was technical and cumbersome working with 16 mm film.

---

2   German filmmaker, author, and photographer.

Even five, ten years later, it became trendy and fashionable to go to film school. And now, of course, the tools that are available to everybody allow you to do the same thing that we were doing in an analog way.

You look at Robert Frank,[3] who's made great documentations of real life on the streets, and it's an epic body of work for its time. But now everybody is doing that in their own way, so what does that mean? I don't know. But, as a filmmaker, it's certainly strange because it's no longer so special, maybe, to make images.

JT: And the question, really, is how can you still recognize beauty if there's so much?

PM: Truthfully, I don't look at a lot of images, and I've become very selective about the films I watch—friends' films, or if I'm working on a jury—but I don't try and see everything that's out there. I don't have the capacity to do it. And so, for me, filmmaking remains a kind of spiritual pursuit of an exploration of our state. But I must say it has become much more complicated. There is such an abundance of things now, it's like, "Well, what am I contributing to the culture, to the world of awareness?"

---

3 Swiss-American documentary filmmaker and photographer known for his 1958 book, *The Americans*, the first edition of which included an introduction by Jack Kerouac.

JT: To seeing.

PM: To seeing. That is the ultimate thing. I think so many problems have at their root a crisis of perception. That's what I'm wrestling with. But it's a crisis of my own perception as well, because I don't have the answers. I'm just a being looking at the world.

JS: Have you always seen film as a medium capable of waking people up? What about when you were younger? Have these themes been present your whole life?

PM: It did start early, even as a young kid, that kind of sensibility. As an only child, I was on my own a lot, and I did creative things when I was young and wanted the space to do that in. I always felt enriched by nature, by watching light, by watching the wind blow, by watching animals—all those things were really meaningful. I think that feeling of presence has always been a high point and something I want to return to regularly. Making films engages you in the intensity and stimulus of production, followed by the isolation of editing, all in an effort to bring the viewer back into those connective states of perception.

I remember when I was a teenager, part of my coming into the world and blossoming was going downtown from the suburbs to visit a dingy art house cinema called Cinema

Lumiere. It was a special and weird place to go. It wasn't part of the mainstream. It was magical. The first films I saw there made me realize the power of cinema and the possibility of deep experience in other worlds. I don't know if that can still happen for a teenager today. I'm sure there are films that speak to you, but given the glut and rapidity of how quickly you can see things on your laptop and how short most of them are and how bitty everything is, I think the chances of being immersed into an experience like that are slimmer.

JS: You have to be receptive to it somehow.

PM: Yeah, so what makes you receptive or not receptive? I guess the risk is that the glut can dull you down.

JS: What I think makes your films quite special is all the different processes that revolve around curiosity. There is that initial spark, but then the ability, and maybe the lack of shame, to actually chase that creative intent, that curiosity, to do something with it. Perhaps that comes out of boredom or some relationship to the void, some relationship to a lack of having everything all the time, or a lack of all the senses being full and overwhelmed. You seem to have the vital faculties surrounding curiosity intact, and you seem to have had them for a long time. Has it been an effort to maintain this freedom to play? Because without that freedom there would never have been *Picture of Light* or any of the other films you've created.

PM: Well yeah, I think the curiosity's just there. It's not something that I try to make happen. It's just there. And the pursuit is fueled by a lot of practical missions to allow it to happen. But it makes you wonder: why not just be? Why not just meditate? Why engage in this very arduous process of tackling and harnessing technology? It's a very complex practice of money and technology and numbers and creativity and language, all for the sake of connecting and seeing.

JS: To be open, to improvise, you have to be curious about what you don't know, what you're feeling, and how to step away from status-quo thinking.

PM: We shot a scene the other day with me playing the piano. I actually hadn't played the piano for a long time. It was interesting how there are those tropes, those patterns that you use again and again that are in you; whether it's in filmmaking or the scales that you play on a piano, or the modes you go after, these are all things that are part of your character that seem unshakeable. And so how do you take the next step knowing that those tropes are there?

The piano was pretty well tuned, but there was one note that was quite off. But that note became very exciting, because it was one note that was not part of the familiar system that had been created for this instrument. I regarded that as one of the things you have to deal with that opens up something new.

JS: That seems to be what you do in your films. In *Picture of Light*, you went north probably not expecting to learn about all the different words for snow but that was like the out-of-tune note amid everything else you had planned.

A lot of your filmmaking seems to be geographic exploration as well. You go on these trips and you find the odd note, and that seems to push you out of predictability. Is that a fair assessment?

PM: It's very interesting that you say I go to places that are not familiar to me. That is a big attraction for sure. It's like I'm going for the note that I don't know. But I've often felt how great it could be to do that in your own hometown, to do that in your place of habit, where all the patterns are happening. It's a challenge. I think I've done that in very minor ways.

JT: Ultimately, it's about being fully open to whatever emerges, to use your craft to look at things, to see them, and then to chronicle what unfolds.

JS: When we were transcribing a lot of the dialogue from your films, especially the ones where you narrate textual pieces that you wrote, I often wondered why you became a filmmaker as opposed to a writer. Why do you think you ended up in film?

PM: Well, because it engages almost everything, and I think as a human being, you're engaged in everything. We speak a language, we see, we hear, we have emotion. I think filmmaking is very attractive as a medium because it replicates so much of that experience, and no one thing to me is more important than the other. Sound is not more important than the image, nor is the image more important than the sound. They have to go together because we experience those things together. But I don't think I would be satisfied just working with words, because it doesn't bring you into an experiential realm in the same way.

JS: Like many of your films, *Picture of Light* seems to explore states of wonder. For example, in the film you say, "I met a man at a dinner who loves to watch the sky. He'd spent as much time watching the sky as I had trying to point cameras and microphones out into the world. It seemed that both of us were trying to find an answer to a question we didn't yet know. As the night closed, we agreed to share a path we had in common: the pursuit of wonder." What does that word mean to you — wonder?

PM: The funny thing is that it crosses through both science and art. I was speaking about Andreas [Züst],[4] my coproducer for the film. He's both a scientist and an artist. And also Albert Hoffman,[5] who I interviewed many years later. His pursuit in chemistry was really one of wonder for the natural world while trying to understand it and to connect to it in a deeper way through the intellect. Wonder is admiration for the beauty and complexity of what we perceive within and around us, and the ability to feel awestruck just by taking it in and being a part of it all. It's a wonderful state, wonder.

JS: Have there been darker or drier periods, periods where the state of wonder was, for whatever reason, not emerging?

PM: Yes, and I would say it's usually when there's a feeling of things being bogged down with problems you can't solve. They could be on an administration level, or a relationship level, or just things that are occupying your presence so

4   Swiss glaciologist (1947–2000), photographer, painter, and patron of the arts.

5   Swiss chemist (1906–2008) and the first to synthesize the compound lysergic acid diethylamide (LSD), in 1938.

much that you don't have room to step out and see them differently. I think many, many, many people are in that state.

js: Perhaps many people enter that state and never get out of it. Would you say you generally feel at peace?

pm: Sometimes, but not on a continual basis. There are deep things, deep currents of things that want to be resolved that are constantly tugging at you, and sometimes they dissipate or become relative. I think that's pretty normal. But that's a hard question, and one I asked people in *Gambling, Gods, and LSD*.[6] Sometimes it's a choice, a personal choice whether to worry about something or let it eat at you, or just see it as an evolving process and feel at peace with it.

But I'd like to ask a question now. Can you tell me what an algorithm is?

js: [laughs] I would say it's human beings trying to extend faculties of thinking into machines. Why do you ask?

pm: Well, because the word is all over the place these days. Little bits I've learned about the stock market being run by algorithms, and I've been considering how a film might be

---

6 *Gambling, Gods, and LSD*, directed by Peter Mettler (Toronto, Canada: Grimthorpe Film, 2002), 35 mm, 180 minutes. Filmed in Canada, the United States, Switzerland, and India.

a kind of algorithm in terms of its early stages of design and planning. Because you're anticipating a future, the finished film, is it an algorithm, the setup that you create to allow things to unfold?

JS: If you look at human thinking in terms of determinism, then you could say that the human mind is an algorithm, no different than a computer. But in my personal thinking, there are two profound differences: a computer algorithm is not curious, and a computer algorithm doesn't feel. These are the differences. And for you to make a film devoid of feeling and curiosity would not be a Peter Mettler film, no matter how hard you try.

It's polemical, because do we really want so much of our society to be run by simulated thinking devoid of curiosity and devoid of feeling? That sounds dystopian to me — whether we're talking about how the stock markets are run, or the music that's being made now according to algorithmic programming, or algorithms telling us what to read.

PM: So an algorithm is strictly something that's found in technological design? It's not found in nature?

JS: That is a very interesting question. Did the original big bang set up an algorithm that determines everything?

PM: Also, a river running its course, hitting rocks and bouncing off, all this cause and effect would be an algorithm, I guess, if you were to recreate that in some kind of technological form. But is it correct to call the river itself an algorithm?

JS: If we want to compare a computer algorithm with nature, we must consider that a lot of the algorithms that are dictating international issues, politics, capitalism, culture and ultimately, the content of human attention, were basically programmed by young men fresh out of Stanford, Harvard, and MIT. So the experience behind these algorithms is basically puberty and then some, whereas the intelligence behind nature goes all the way back to the big bang. I mean, even hydrogen and helium had a lot of time to commingle and figure out how they would get on, something we can't say about the most powerful algorithms now dictating our lives and the fate of our planet.

PM: It's interesting to look at the evolution. We invent the car, we invent the washing machine; we invent tools to make life easier. Then we develop the Internet and e-mail, and all these things we hope will simplify life, but then the algorithm takes it into a whole other level. It's like, "Okay, now we don't have to touch it anymore." Now it's actually affecting the course of evolution. It has a life of its own, contrary to a line in *Picture of Light*: "Technology doesn't yet have a life of its own." And it also prompts questions I explore about what "nature" is in my more recent films — *The End of Time*[7] and *Becoming Animal*.[8]

JS: Doesn't that frighten you?

PM: Yeah. From a personal perspective it feels like we may lose something of the treasured wonder we are familiar with. It's hard to say what will come next but our species, if it continues to exist at all, likely won't even remember what once was.

JS: The evolution from analog technology to digital is also interesting. For artists, both are tools of representation, as is speech or a cave painting. But analog maintains at least some connection to nature and physicality. Recording sound or image on analog media is an organic process, whereas digital technology is no different than the cloning of an organism.

---

7 *The End of Time*, directed by Peter Mettler (Toronto, Canada: Grimthorpe Film, 2012), DCP, 110 minutes. Filmed in Canada, Hawaii, Switzerland, and India.

8 *Becoming Animal*, directed by Emma Davie and Peter Mettler (Zurich, Switzerland: Maximage, 2018), DCP, 78 minutes. Filmed in Grand Teton National Park, Wyoming, United States.

PM: The different processes retain a different connection to the original experience, yeah.

I don't know if I told you about my encounter with the Kogi[9] people who have invited me to go up the mountain. I'm thinking seriously about shooting something there on analog film for these kinds of reasons.

JS: Is filmstock still available? You've shared with us in the past some of the benefits of digital filmmaking, and yet you're talking about possibly doing this new project on film. Why?

PM: Well, the Kogi live in—for lack of a better word—an analog world. I think as part of meeting them and sharing an experience with them, it could be more in tune to have that direct relationship with the emulsion being exposed by light; that that is the artifact that we're looking at, as opposed to the translation of light into numbers and numbers back into light. I have a sense that they work with energy and light and growth and nature; so it just seems appropriate.

---

9 An indigenous group living in northern Colombia. In spite of the Spanish invasion of that country in the late fifteenth and sixteenth centuries, a period when most indigenous peoples of Colombia were converted or enslaved, the Kogi managed to preserve their culture within the isolated mountain ranges of Sierra Nevada de Santa Marta.

JT: With an analog camera, you'd be looking differently, because you won't have unlimited hours to shoot. So you would be much more aware, perhaps, of the preciousness of the material.

JS: And there won't be any screens or menus to distract you. Your early films were shot on film, and now, like most or all filmmakers, you're shooting on digital. Don't the screens and menus change your perception of what you're seeing and how you film?

PM: I've spent the last two years with my current camera dealing with exactly what you're talking about. It comes with a flip-out screen. The ergonomics on the motion of the zoom, on the aperture, where the controls are, it's all very digital. There's a huge menu of settings, but you can lose the sensitivity and physicality of shooting and moving and seeing, because of all the electronic translations.

JS: Carrying around a trunk full of film reels is probably not so easy, but the act of filming on an analog camera seems limited to drastically fewer technical distractions compared with a digital camera.

Surely changes in technology mirror the people making and using those technologies. Maybe all these screens and menus reflect our own increased mental agitation. Maybe digital art mirrors our time. Digital creative tools brought us hyperreal resolution, but also unlimited options for manipulating reality. Now we have both the tools and the desire.

The Internet is the wet dream of humanity. Now, for the first time in human history, we have at our disposal the option to remain in a relatively disembodied state all the time, in a state of distraction and fragmentation, in this disembodied virtual world that resembles life, this representational world, without really having to feel much. Perhaps this is what we've always wanted. The desire is not new; it's ancient. We just never before had the technology to actually obtain it.

PM: I guess the question is whether filmmaking perpetuates direct, unmediated experience or disconnects us from the "real" world.

JS: Is it perpetuating direct experience or sleep or wakefulness? All are possible. But the ability for someone to portray, artfully, all the things beyond logic that are so unique to human beings, the things that are beyond the algorithm—imagination, empathy, curiosity, creativity, love—these are the things that make life worth living. Without those faculties, we have mediocrity, we have war, we have fragmentation, et cetera. This is also the difference between art and commodity, and a film can be either.

PM: But isn't there a paradox in the fact that it's a film that's waking you, pointing you to direct experience, as opposed to direct experience itself?

JS: Of course it's a paradox, which is simply to say that to critique technology doesn't mean that all technology is bad. That is the number one point of confusion we get when we talk to people about Analog Sea, this assumption that we're saying technology is bad. No, no, no. The right kind of technology in the right moment is the right thing, just like medicine.

PM: Earlier we were talking about making films now versus making films before, and I do wrestle with the notion of contributing to this huge glut of image experiences today. It's just not that easy anymore to create something for a space like Cinema Lumiere—incidentally now an electronics store around the corner from where I live—nor to have the distribution for projected cinema experiences to happen.

It's not just the system of distribution and financing and TV and all that, it's also a matter of drawing the people into the cinema in the first place. And once they're there, are they even capable of looking at something that suggests direct experience, because they're so used to YouTube and such? Just to show something without an edit in it for two minutes is, I find, very suspenseful, but many people now find such a long cut completely radical and intolerable, even unwatchable.

JT: As more people become numb to subtlety, artists and film studios feel they need more sensationalism, more speed to reach the audience where they're at. To balance all of this, I think it's vital that we continue to have transformative art.

JS: Ultimately, all art is representation. Before that first film of the train frightening the audience, as you mention in *Picture of Light*, or before the first photograph, or the first live radio broadcast, there were other forms of representation—painting and speech itself. The issue is what is being represented and whether it's a finger pointing the observer toward or away from the direct experience that awaits them outside of the theater or the silence beyond the off button.

PM: Good answer.

JS: How much are you struggling with it? The glut? Is it something you're thinking about? For example, have you ever thought about quitting making films?

PM: Yes, pretty much after every film I've made. [laughs] Because it's a weird thing to do. It's a very strange engagement with reality, and it profoundly affects you. But it does seem to me worthwhile, like stepping into a wide-open and immensely mysterious dancehall and using whatever tools you have to understand the nature of the dance.

They Call That a Tree
Pema Chödrön

I heard a story about Trungpa Rinpoche sitting in a garden with His Holiness Dilgo Khyentse Rinpoche. People were standing around at a distance, close enough to hear but far enough away to give them privacy and space. It was a beautiful day. These two gentlemen had been sitting in the garden for a long time, just sitting there not saying anything. Time went on, and they just sat in the garden not saying anything and seeming to enjoy it very much. Then Trungpa Rinpoche broke the silence and began to laugh. He said to Dilgo Khyentse Rinpoche, pointing across the lawn, "They call that a tree." Whereupon Khyentse Rinpoche started to laugh too.

Pema Chödrön, *Start Where You Are: A Guide to Compassionate Living* (Boston: Shambhala, 1994), pp. 25–26.

Glow
James Lasdun

There is something at once mind-blowing and unas-similable about the phenomenon. The aurora borealis is, in Karl Ove Knausgård's phrase, "immensely foreign," and it puts you into a kind of panic in which you want to simultaneously observe it, describe it, rejoice in it, interpret it, and record it. Nothing you've learned or read about the subject — scientific, folkloric, touristic — seems remotely adequate or even relevant to the experience. You develop the overwhelming impression that some cryptic but staggeringly powerful intelligence is staging a performance expressly for you, even as you remind yourself that this can't be the case. Surprisingly intense emotions grip you.

James Lasdun, "Glow: Chasing the Aurora Borealis," *The New Yorker* (April 29, 2019), p. 47.

Aurora from Space
Don L. Lind

Imagine the earth, surrounded by its magnetic field, orbiting in the atmosphere of the sun. The upper corona is a supersonic wind that is expanding and blows past the earth, and the earth is actually in that wind. And that sweeps the magnetic field around the earth into a long tail, and the residual magnetic field is called the magnetosphere, or the magnetic tail. If the magnetic field were visible, the earth would look like a tremendous comet with a tail that goes way out past the moon. As the solar wind sweeps along the sides of this magnetic field, it generates energy that is dumped into the tail. And then every once in a while, by some impulsive mechanism that we don't quite understand yet, that energy is dumped down the magnetic field lines into the earth and hits the earth in two circles, one around the north magnetic pole and one around the south magnetic pole. That constitutes the aurora.

And what you're looking at is, first of all, the moonlit clouds below us and a bright streak of light in the sky which is just one filament of this great circle that surrounds the south geomagnetic pole; and then there's the mirror image of that in the northern hemisphere. And you're looking at the stream of particles from the magnetosphere, which is actually exciting the atoms in the atmosphere to glow. When you look down at that aurora you really see an impressive scene. The electrical current surging through that aurora is on average about the same energy as the entire network of high-tension power lines in North America—Bonneville Dam and Hoover Dam and all the rest of the power lines put together. The bottom of that curtain is about seventy miles in the air, and we're about one hundred ninety miles up, so we're looking down on the top of it, which is sweeping past the aurora at 17,500 miles an hour ... and as the magnetic tail, or the magnetosphere, shimmers and shakes and jiggles, it changes the pattern of that aurora. But more importantly, this magnetosphere is the environment in which we live and we simply need to understand it.

Spacelab 3 mission launched the Orbiter Challenger from the Kennedy Space Center in Florida on April 29, 1985. Among a variety of scientific experiments on this mission was one developed by Dr. Lind to take unique three-dimensional video recordings of the earth's aurora. After completing a hundred and ten orbits of the earth and traveling just under three million miles, the space shuttle landed on May 6, 1985.

Adapted from a 1985 interview with Don L. Lind filmed in space and featured in *Picture of Light*, directed by Peter Mettler (Toronto, Canada: Grimthorpe Film, 1994), 35 mm, 83 minutes.

Art and Science
Albert Einstein

Where the world ceases to be a stage for personal hopes, aspirations, and desires, and we stand before it as free creatures, full of admirations, questions, and contemplation, we enter the realm of art and science. If we describe what we see and experience in the language of logic, we do science; if we convey connections through forms that are inaccessible to the rational mind, but intuitively recognizable as making sense, we do art.

Albert Einstein, "The Common Element in Artistic and Scientific Experience," in *The Collected Papers of Albert Einstein*, Vol. 7, *The Berlin Years: Writings 1918–1921* (Princeton: Princeton University Press, 2002), p. 207.

Interview with Andreas Buchleitner
Jonathan Simons

The German city of Freiburg is known for its wine and intellectuals. Erasmus in the sixteenth century, Max Weber in the late nineteenth, and Hannah Arendt in the 1920s all spent time thinking and writing in this green jewel of a city edging the forest. With France to the west, Basel and the Swiss Alps to the south, and the *Schwarzwald*, one of Germany's largest forests, to the east and north, Freiburg and its university continue to be a tonic shelter for the slow practice of scientific and philosophical inquiry.

In the middle of this haven stands a nondescript ten-story Post-war Modern construction favorably known as the "Physics High-rise." The original 1950s elevator links together ten floors of approximately one hundred and forty physicists, all of whom spend their days questioning the sometimes predictable but often strange behavior of energy and matter. What a pleasure it was meeting one of them.

Born in Munich during the Cold War, Dr. Andreas Buchleitner was awarded his PhD in physics from Pierre and Marie Curie University in Paris, was an associate professor at the Max Planck Institute, and is now professor of theoretical physics at the Albert Ludwig University of Freiburg, where he teaches and researches quantum optics and quantum computing.

My visit with Andreas began in silence as we stood at his ninth-floor window, gazing down like birds to the historical city center below and on to the Schlossberg mountain and forest beyond.

JONATHAN SIMONS: My first impression coming here, and you can tell me if I'm wrong, is that you've managed to escape the marketplace. You're up here with your students engaging curiosity, being intellectually playful, while everyone else is worried about branding, advertising, and selling products.

ANDREAS BUCHLEITNER: Yeah, that's a serious problem. Often when I come here I say to myself, "*Ich erhole mich*" —I'm recovering. That's because with my students, I can focus entirely on science, not on branding. But of course, there's another debate entirely, and an unpleasant one: if everything in life falls into the realm of economics, under which conditions can you do good science?

Now, for instance, alongside quantum science or quantum computing, there's also the field of artificial intelligence, or AI. In our computer science department, there are more and more people studying AI, and in quantum physics ever more people talk of quantum machine learning. Certainly the majority of people wouldn't know what that means. Very often it's a question of branding—old wine, new bottles. There is a very strong economic pull, and this sets the boundary conditions.

In Germany, we are still relatively privileged because the German constitution guarantees freedom of research and teaching, but we have to make use of this privilege. If we don't use it, they will take it away. For me as a theorist this is easier than for an experimentalist, because the experimentalist depends far more on funding. I depend on funding too, but I also depend on sufficiently intelligent people. In the end, as long as I have chalk and the blackboard and three very good students, I can compete with anybody in the world, at least in one field.

JS: So what are the conditions required for you and your students to perform well? And are those conditions the same as the conditions for an artist or a poet to perform well?

AB: Ah! Very good question. When students and I debate about general science matters, I often bring up the hypothesis that being a scientist is in many respects similar to being an artist. The most important condition is having people with whom one can talk constructively and critically. People have to be ready to fight for their own well-reasoned perspectives.

Then there is time. In high school, I took a course on art history that discussed *vita contemplativa* and *vita activa*. Nowadays, almost nobody speaks about *vita contemplativa*.

That's why I was so pleasantly surprised to read Han's essay in the last issue of *The Analog Sea Review*.[1] Yet if I brought copies to my friends here, they would look at me as if to say, "What do you mean? This isn't productive."

JS: It's that kind of time you're talking about, isn't it? Contemplative time. Time without the pressures of appeasing others or the stress of commerce. You have to worry about funding, but that's only half the battle, right? Once you get funding, then you have time. And what do you do with the time?

AB: Depends. My favorite occupation is working with the students and teaching, discussing in detail what has been done and what should be done next. This is the heart of my job. But if I had more time, I would probably read more. Twenty years ago as a postdoc, when I started to run my own group, I had much more time because I had no institutional responsibilities. I knew every piece of literature written in the areas in which we were working. Now you see an increase in apparent scientific production in terms of pages printed; I stress "apparent" because there is not necessarily more substance. Nowadays, even if I had more time, I would

---

1 Byung-Chul Han, "Vita Contemplativa," *The Analog Sea Review*, no. 1 (June 2018), pp. 69–83.

not be able to read everything because the volume of papers published is too large — which, in principle, undermines the scientific method.

JS: Why is that? Because there's too much material?

AB: Yeah, too much material. It's a principle: as scientists, we need actual scientific discourse, otherwise everybody's talking and nobody's listening anymore. This happens everywhere, but in science I think it's particularly harmful because we want to learn; otherwise, we just reiterate what we've been doing for the last twenty years. Therefore, when I say I would use the time for reading, I mean I would use it to read in breadth — not just to read what I need for publishing the next paper, but also to get new ideas by reading something which I'm not yet familiar with, or from which I would like to learn something new. For this at least, I need time to think.

   To the first and second generation of my students, I used to say, "Reserve at least half a day a week where you just go to the library and don't do anything else. Read the important periodicals, scan what has been done in the area you might be interested in, and go through the articles and try to understand what they do." So they took the time, and it required a physical effort: they would go to a library in another building, where they would be cut off from the phone and wouldn't see e-mails coming in. Nowadays it's more difficult for students to truly concentrate, and I think this is a matter of the conditions under which they grew up.

JS: What if you had a student who was distracted every two or three minutes, or even every twenty minutes? Would you have hope for that student?

AB: This is a difficult question, because on the one hand I think it's clear that I can concentrate or focus better on something than they can. On the other hand, I often see them sitting at the computer with headphones on, looking at multiple screens, and some of them still do very good work.

JS: This topic of conditions is fascinating. When I think about the conditions I need to write, first I need silence; not for any romantic reason, but because writing has its own musicality in the way the words move in my mind. Would you say that thinking about complex mathematics and problems in physics requires similar conditions?

AB: For sure. When I want to write a proper equation, typically I withdraw. I go to a place where nobody can disturb me, and I tend to get … not necessarily unpleasant, but it's very clear that I'm unhappy when I'm disturbed, because I have to concentrate very deeply to do good work, whether I'm working on some mathematical structure or on any text longer than half a page.

JS: So on the one hand you're saying that maybe your younger students have a different way of engaging their intelligence. Maybe they've developed their own ways of dealing with a diversity of information coming at the same time. But you're also saying that to get at a problem, you have to go deep into it.

AB: Yes. I think that's true for the students, and I think it's worse for young postdocs in particular; they feel pressure to get a job, so of course they will try to adapt their ways of thinking to what they believe is expected of them. But if every scientist had the same motivation, their work would not be very original; it would just be industrial production. That's why stubbornness, I think, is a very important quality.

JS: I imagine there's a whole universe behind what you mean by the word "stubbornness." It seems to me that you're talking about not cutting corners, not being lazy, caring about the details. These questions of mastery over your material, the depth that you can achieve within your discoveries, these are terms that are talked about in the arts but also in depth psychology in terms of individuation.

Within science, there's increasingly a collective lust for the computers to do our thinking. Isn't that the opposite of the stubbornness that you're referring to?

AB: Precisely. I think of individuation in particular, because I'm not interested in making clones. I'm bored enough if I look in the mirror! For example, when a PhD begins, we suggest a research topic for the candidate. But at some point, ideally about halfway through the doctorate, the candidate says, "Andreas, this is what you're interested in, but it's not good enough. I'm actually interested in this, and I have sound reasons why." And then we will fight. We have to fight—not just because I'm the professor so of course I must be right [laughs], but for the sake of having the argument. This is the purpose of the PhD.

In my opinion, we at university are here for the rare events. Progress in science, as in art, is achieved by those people who do something extraordinary—that which, by definition, cannot be standardized. If I want to standardize something, I have to have a picture of how the product looks. But I'm doing science because I'm after results which I cannot yet imagine. This is the difference.

JS: Can we talk about light?

AB: Sure.

JS: What do we not know about light?

AB: That is an interesting question. Actually, in principle I would say that we understand light very well. At least, put on the spot like this, I wouldn't say there's any truly important open question about the nature of light.

JS: So it's other subatomic particles that are the core mystery in physics.

AB: Well, light is a field, a wave phenomenon. But if you go quantum, at some point you see the wave–particle duality: these waves have a granular structure, so they also behave like particles, like photons. These are just small bunches of energy that, when they interact, change the state of matter. What we detect is the change of matter.

JS: But when the human eye is looking at it, it behaves differently.

AB: This is a very widespread misunderstanding. Whether we look or not does not matter. People often endow quantum mechanics with this mystification. When they hear "observer," they think of course of a conscious observer. Actually, the observer is just another object with which the quantum object is interacting; whether this other object is alive or not doesn't matter. You don't really have that wave–particle duality in the eye. What happens is that the photon coming in is absorbed by a molecule. The molecule is brought into another electronic state, and this then triggers an electronic current in your brain that tells your nerves there is light.

JS: Have you ever seen the aurora borealis?

AB: Yes. I went to Finland for a scientific meeting a couple of years ago, and I finally saw it.

JS: As a physicist who focuses on optics, what was your experience? What were your thoughts? Was it an experience of science or of poetry?

AB: Poetry, of course. I mean, it's just beautiful. Like a rainbow: it's an extremely beautiful phenomenon. In principle I understand scientifically what the aurora borealis is, but that's quite irrelevant. I wasn't looking at the sky because I wanted to verify my equations. I'm not sure that scientists differ here from artists. I think science, like theology or art, trains you to be more attentive to the details of the surrounding world, a little more open to simply watching things.

JS: It makes us realize that we're living in a situation where we don't have to optimize and manufacture life in order to experience beauty.

AB: Yeah, it's clear that beauty needs no manufacturing. For example, I went to the Sinai, which is mostly a rocky desert. I stayed there for ten days or so, typically sleeping under the open sky. The light changes so much from sunrise to night. It's just amazing. And in the valleys, depending on the iron content, you get different colors. I really couldn't believe that the landscape was not manmade [laughs]. I had to approach the rocks closely and see.

JS: What have you discovered that's most interesting about the mechanics of light?

AB: In our work, we think a lot about certain structural elements of light; in particular—when I make faint light with few photons—how the interplay of these photons affects the phenomenology of light, which I witness as an experimentalist. This can result in very interesting, complex structures. But the complex phenomena we are after are not so much grounded in the very nature of light, but rather on the next level, when we put the base constituents of light together under specific experimental conditions.

Recently I was talking to a philosopher, and he brought up the concept of the *ontological primitive*.[2] A photon, to me, is probably the neatest ontological primitive we have. Therefore, I think about how I can create complexity with light, and how I can use light to study certain non-trivial properties of complex systems.

Do you know the story about the *Schildbürger*—the people from Schilda? This is a popular German fairy tale of simple-minded people who do all kinds of strange things. At some point, for example, they build a new town hall, but then realize they forgot to build windows, so it's dark inside. They say, "What can we do? Let's take big sacks, go outside, open the sacks, get the sunlight in, close the sacks, and bring them into the building so it will be bright." This is just one of the strange ideas these people have which obviously cannot work.

JS: Capturing light.

AB: Actually, in physics we can do this today. We can build cavities that we can make completely dark so we can prove when a photon enters. It's not so easy to make a room completely dark; typically you always have a couple of photons.

---

2 An *ontological primitive* is an entity or a concept which exists or is well defined independently of other entities or concepts.

Then instead of taking sacks, we take atoms, put them in an excited state, send them in there, and arrange things such that they release the excitation as a photon and end up in a ground state. The photon can stay there for almost a second, which is a very satisfying experimental achievement. In dark rooms with no light source, we can essentially switch on the light.

This shows that nowadays we have very high control of single constituents of matter. Serge Haroche[3] was awarded the Nobel Prize for doing these kinds of experiments controlling single constituents of light matter.

JS: What would you say if one of your graduate students had a moment of significant doubt and said, "Why am I spending all my life on these questions when computers will soon solve them in half a second?"

AB: I don't see evidence that there will be a computer which does that. All of us have doubts sometimes about why we are sitting here working on these kinds of problems. In math, for example, there are people bringing up the idea that you can use AI to check the validity of mathematical proofs, and this probably is possible — for example, a prime

---

3 French physicist awarded the 2012 Nobel Prize for Physics for his work on the manipulation of single photons.

factorization of a big number. I believe that you can build algorithms so that a computer does that for you, but I don't believe that this represents the heart of human creativity.

It seems to me closely related to the question of free will. I'm in favor of the hypothesis that we have free will. And I have the impression that, if we are capable of creative acts, we achieve things which could not be anticipated—rare events. It's very difficult to train algorithms to do so because we have not seen enough to gather sufficient data. I can simulate all kinds of things, but the probability of a computer replicating what a human brain might create is very small. These events, these rare events, in my opinion, are the evidence for what I would call creativity.

Surrogate Moon
Jerry Mander

When you are watching television the major thing you are doing is looking at light. The philosopher John Brockman[1] was the first person to put it that way to me, remarking that this in itself represents an enormous change in human experience. For four hours a day, human beings sit in dark rooms, their bodies stilled, gazing at light. Nothing like this has ever happened before.

Previous generations, millions of them, looked at starlight, firelight and moonlight, and there is no doubt that these experiences stir important feelings. There are cultures that spent time gazing at the sun, but there is no culture in all of history that has spent such enormous blocks of time, all of the people together, every day, sitting in dark rooms looking at artificial light.

Anne Waldman,[2] the poet, has suggested that television might itself represent a surrogate moon; a substitute for the original experience for which we, somewhere, continue to long. If true, this might be merely poignant if it weren't for

---

1 American author, literary agent, and one-time Andy Warhol collaborator. —*Ed*.

2 American poet who, in 1974, co-founded, with Allen Ginsberg, the Jack Kerouac School of Disembodied Poetics at Naropa Institute in Boulder, Colorado. —*Ed*.

some important distinctions between looking at the moon or a fire and looking at television.

Television light is purposeful and directed rather than ambient. It is projected into our eyes from behind the screen by cathode-ray guns which are literally aimed at us. These guns are powered by 25,000 volts in the case of color television, and about 15,000 volts in black-and-white sets.

The guns shoot electron streams at phosphors on the screen. This makes the phosphors glow, and their light projects from the screen into our eyes. It is not quite accurate to say that when we watch television we are looking at light; it is more accurate to say that light is projected into us. We are *receiving* light through our eyes into our bodies, far enough in to affect our endocrine system. Some physicists say that the eye does not distinguish between ambient light, which has reflected off other surfaces, and directed light, which comes straight at the eye, undeterred, but others think the difference is important.

There is another hot debate in physics on the question of whether light is particulate matter or wave energy. For our purposes, however, what needs to be appreciated is that whether light is matter or energy it is a *thing* which is entering us. When you are watching television, you are experiencing something like lines of energy passing from cathode gun to phosphor through your eyes into your body. You are as connected to the television set as your arm would be to the electrical current in the wall—about which there is the same question of wave versus particle—if you had stuck a knife into the socket.

These are not metaphors. There is a concentrated passage of energy from machine to you, and none in the reverse. In this sense, the machine is literally dominant, and you are passive.

Jerry Mander, *Four Arguments for the Elimination of Television* (New York: Quill, 1978), pp. 170–171.

Of the Air
Mary Mercier

They do not gather into barns
or malls. They have no need for text
nor engineers to reinvent the gyroscope.
They fly through clouds without a license,
never mistaking up for down. And nothing holds
them back except the long and vacant hours before dawn.
Then morning rinses wings with light. Theirs
the kingdom and the glory that erases night,
theirs the emptiness of air.

The Machine Stops
Oliver Sacks

My favorite aunt, Auntie Len, when she was in her eighties, told me that she had not had too much difficulty adjusting to all the things that were new in her lifetime—jet planes, space travel, plastics, and so on—but she could not accustom herself to the disappearance of the old. "Where have all the horses gone?" she would sometimes say. Born in 1892, she had grown up in a London full of carriages and horses.

I have similar feelings myself. A few years ago, I was walking with my niece Liz down Mill Lane, a road near the house in London where I grew up. I stopped at a railway bridge where I had loved leaning over the railings as a child. I watched various electric and diesel trains go by, and after a few minutes Liz, growing impatient, asked, "What are you waiting for?" I said that I was waiting for a steam train. Liz looked at me as if I were crazy.

"Uncle Oliver," she said. "There haven't been steam trains for more than forty years."

I have not adjusted as well as my aunt to some aspects of the new—perhaps because the rate of social change associated with technological advances has been so rapid and profound. I cannot get used to seeing myriads of people in the street peering into little boxes or holding them in front of their faces, walking blithely in the path of moving traffic, totally out of touch with their surroundings. I am most alarmed by such distraction and inattention when I see young parents staring at their cell phones and ignoring their own babies as they walk or wheel them along. Such children, unable to attract their parents' attention, must feel neglected, and they will surely show the effects of this in the years to come.

In his 2007 novel *Exit Ghost,* Philip Roth speaks of how radically changed New York City appears to a reclusive writer who has been away from it for a decade. He is forced to overhear cell-phone conversations all around him, and he wonders, "What had happened in these ten years for there suddenly to be so much to say — so much so pressing that it couldn't wait to be said? ... I did not see how anyone could believe he was continuing to live a human existence by walking about talking into his phone for half his waking life."

These gadgets, already ominous in 2007, have now immersed us in a virtual reality far denser, more absorbing, and even more dehumanizing.

I am confronted every day with the complete disappearance of the old civilities. Social life, street life, and attention to people and things around one have largely disappeared, at least in big cities, where a majority of the population is now glued almost without pause to their phones or other devices — jabbering, texting, playing computer games, turning more and more to virtual reality of every sort.

Everything is public now, potentially: one's thoughts, one's photos, one's movements, one's purchases. There is no privacy and apparently little desire for it in a world devoted to nonstop use of social media. Every minute, every second, has to be spent with one's device clutched in one's hand. Those trapped in this virtual world are never alone, never able to concentrate and appreciate in their own way, silently. They have given up, to a great extent, the amenities and achievements of civilization: solitude and leisure, the sanction to be oneself, truly absorbed, whether in contemplating a work of art, a scientific theory, a sunset, or the face of one's beloved.

A few years ago, I was invited to join a panel discussion titled "Information and Communication in the Twenty-First Century." One of the panelists, an Internet pioneer, said proudly that his young daughter surfed the Internet twelve hours a day and had access to a breadth and range of information that no one of a previous generation could have imagined. I asked whether she had read any of Jane Austen's novels, or *any* classic novel, and he said, "No, she doesn't have time for anything like that." I wondered aloud whether she would then have no solid understanding of human nature or society, and suggested that while she might be stocked with wide-ranging information, that was different from knowledge; she would have a mind both shallow and centerless. Half the audience cheered; the other half booed.

Much of this, remarkably, was envisaged by E. M. Forster in his 1909 short story "The Machine Stops," in which he imagined a future where people live underground in isolated cells, never seeing one another and communicating only by audio and visual devices. In this world, original thought and direct observation are discouraged—"Beware of first-hand ideas!" people are told. Humanity has been overtaken by "the Machine," which provides all comforts and meets all needs—except the need for human contact. One young man, Kuno, pleads with his mother via a Skype-like technology, "I want to see you not through the Machine. I want to speak to you not through the wearisome Machine."

He says to his mother, who is absorbed in her hectic, meaningless life, "We have lost the sense of space. … We have lost a part of ourselves. … Cannot you see … that it is we that are dying, and that down here the only thing that really lives is the Machine?"

This is how I feel increasingly often about our bewitched, besotted society, too.

AS ONE'S DEATH GROWS NEAR, one may take comfort in the feeling that life will go on—if not for oneself then for one's children, or for what one has created. Here at least one can invest hope, though there may be no hope for oneself physically and (for those of us who are not believers) no sense of any "spiritual" survival after bodily death.

But it may not be enough to create, to contribute, to have influenced others, if one feels, as I do now, that the very culture in which one was nourished and to which one had given one's best in return is itself threatened. Though I am supported and stimulated by my friends, by readers around the world, by memories of my life, and by the joy that writing gives me, I have, as many of us must have, deep fears about the well-being and even survival of our world.

Such fears have been expressed at the highest intellectual and moral levels. Martin Rees, Astronomer Royal and former president of the Royal Society, is not a man given to apocalyptic thinking, but in 2003 he published a book called *Our Final Hour,* subtitled *A Scientist's Warning—How Terror, Error, and Environmental Disaster Threaten Humankind's Future in This Century.* More recently, Pope Francis published his remarkable encyclical *Laudato Si',* a deep consideration not only of human-induced climate change and widespread ecological disaster but of the desperate state of the poor and the growing threats of consumerism and misuse of technology. Traditional wars have now been joined by genocide, extremism, and terrorism and, in some cases, by the deliberate destruction of our human heritage, of history and culture itself.

These threats of course concern me, but at a distance — I worry more about the subtle, pervasive draining out of meaning, of intimate contact, from our society and culture.

When I was eighteen, I read Hume for the first time; I was horrified by the vision he expressed in his 1738 *Treatise of Human Nature,* in which he wrote that mankind is "nothing but a bundle or collection of different perceptions, which succeed each other with an inconceivable rapidity, and are in a perpetual flux and movement." As a neurologist, I have seen many patients rendered amnesic by destruction of the memory systems in their brains, and I cannot help feeling that these people, having lost any sense of a past or a future and caught in a flutter of ephemeral, ever-changing sensations, have in some way been reduced from human beings to Humean ones.

I have only to venture into the streets of my own neighborhood, the West Village, to see such Humean casualties by the thousand: younger people, for the most part, who have grown up in our social-media era, have no personal memory of how things were before, and no immunity to the seductions of digital life. What we are seeing — and bringing on ourselves — resembles a neurological catastrophe on a gigantic scale.

Nonetheless, I dare to hope that, despite everything, human life and its richness of cultures will survive, even on a ravaged earth. While some see art as a bulwark of our culture, our collective memory, I see science, with its depth of thought, its palpable achievements and potentials, as equally important; and science, good science, is flourishing as never before, moving cautiously and slowly, its insights checked by continual self-testing and experimentation. Though I revere good writing and art and music, it seems to me that only science, aided by human decency, common sense, farsightedness, and concern for the unfortunate and the poor, offers the world any hope in its present morass. This idea is explicit in Pope Francis's encyclical and may be practiced not only with vast, centralized technologies but by workers, artisans, and farmers in the villages of the world. Between us, we can surely pull the world through its present crises and lead the way to a happier time ahead. As I face my own impending departure from the world, I have to believe in this—that mankind and our planet will survive, that life will continue, and that this will not be our final hour.

This essay, originally titled "Life Continues," was first published in Oliver Sacks's final collection of essays, *Everything in its Place: First Loves and Lost Tales* (New York: Alfred A. Knopf, 2019). Dr. Sacks died in 2015.

Buttons and Switches
E. M. Forster

There were buttons and switches everywhere—buttons to call for food, for music, for clothing. There was the hot-bath button, by pressure of which a basin of (imitation) marble rose out of the floor, filled to the brim with a warm deodorized liquid. There was the cold-bath button. There was the button that produced literature. And there were of course the buttons by which she communicated with her friends. The room, though it contained nothing, was in touch with all that she cared for in the world.

E. M. Forster, "The Machine Stops," in *The Eternal Moment and Other Stories* (New York: Harcourt, Brace & Company, 1928), p. 20.

Docile Cows
Yuval Noah Harari

Currently, humans risk becoming similar to domesticated animals. We have bred docile cows that produce enormous amounts of milk but are otherwise far inferior to their wild ancestors. They are less agile, less curious, and less resourceful. We are now creating tame humans who produce enormous amounts of data and function as efficient chips in a huge data-processing mechanism, but they hardly maximize their human potential. If we are not careful, we will end up with downgraded humans misusing upgraded computers to wreak havoc on themselves and on the world.

Yuval Noah Harari, "Why Technology Favors Tyranny," *The Atlantic* (October 2018), p. 70.

The Technocratic Paradigm
Pope Francis

It can be said that many problems of today's world stem from the tendency, at times unconscious, to make the method and aims of science and technology an epistemological paradigm which shapes the lives of individuals and the workings of society. The effects of imposing this model on reality as a whole, human and social, are seen in the deterioration of the environment, but this is just one sign of a reductionism which affects every aspect of human and social life. We have to accept that technological products are not neutral, for they create a framework which ends up conditioning lifestyles and shaping social possibilities along the lines dictated by the interests of certain powerful groups. Decisions which may seem purely instrumental are in reality decisions about the kind of society we want to build.

The idea of promoting a different cultural paradigm and employing technology as a mere instrument is nowadays inconceivable. The technological paradigm has become so dominant that it would be difficult to do without its resources and even more difficult to utilize them without being dominated by their internal logic. It has become countercultural to choose a lifestyle whose goals are even partly independent of technology, of its costs and its power to globalize and make us all the same. Technology tends to absorb everything into its ironclad logic, and those who are surrounded with technology "know full well that it moves forward in the final analysis neither for profit nor for the well-being of the human race," that "in the most radical sense of the term power is its motive—a lordship over all."[1] As a result, "man seizes hold of the naked elements of both nature and human nature."[2] Our capacity to make decisions, a more genuine freedom and the space for each one's alternative creativity are diminished.

THE SPECIALIZATION WHICH BELONGS TO technology makes it difficult to see the larger picture. The fragmentation of knowledge proves helpful for concrete applications, and yet it often leads to a loss of appreciation for the whole, for the relationships between things, and for the broader horizon, which then becomes irrelevant. This very fact makes it hard to find adequate ways of solving the more complex problems of today's world, particularly those regarding the environment and the poor; these problems cannot be dealt with from a single perspective or from a single set of interests. A science which would offer solutions to the great issues would necessarily have to take into account the data generated by other fields of knowledge, including philosophy and

---

1 Romano Guardini, *The End of the Modern World* (Chicago: Regnery Publishing, 1968), p. 74.

2 Ibid., p. 74.

social ethics; but this is a difficult habit to acquire today. Nor are there genuine ethical horizons to which one can appeal. Life gradually becomes a surrender to situations conditioned by technology, itself viewed as the principal key to the meaning of existence. In the concrete situation confronting us, there are a number of symptoms which point to what is wrong, such as environmental degradation, anxiety, a loss of the purpose of life and of community living. Once more we see that "realities are more important than ideas."[3]

THERE IS ALSO THE FACT that people no longer seem to believe in a happy future; they no longer have blind trust in a better tomorrow based on the present state of the world and our technical abilities. There is a growing awareness that scientific and technological progress cannot be equated with the progress of humanity and history, a growing sense that the way to a better future lies elsewhere. This is not to reject the possibilities which technology continues to offer us. But humanity has changed profoundly, and the accumulation of constant novelties exalts a superficiality which pulls us in one direction. It becomes difficult to pause and recover depth in life. If architecture reflects the spirit of an age, our megastructures and drab apartment blocks express the spirit

---

3 Pope Francis, "Realities Are More Important Than Ideas," *Apostolic Exhortation: Evangelii Gaudium* (November 24, 2013), p. 231.

of globalized technology, where a constant flood of new products coexists with a tedious monotony. Let us refuse to resign ourselves to this, and continue to wonder about the purpose and meaning of everything. Otherwise we would simply legitimate the present situation and need new forms of escapism to help us endure the emptiness.

All of this shows the urgent need for us to move forward in a bold cultural revolution. Science and technology are not neutral; from the beginning to the end of a process, various intentions and possibilities are in play and can take on distinct shapes. Nobody is suggesting a return to the Stone Age, but we do need to slow down and look at reality in a different way, to appropriate the positive and sustainable progress which has been made, but also to recover the values and the great goals swept away by our unrestrained delusions of grandeur.

Excerpted from Pope Francis, "The Globalization of the Technocratic Paradigm," in *Laudato Si* (Vatican City: Vatican Press, 2015), pp. 80–86. Originally published in Latin and translated by the Vatican Press into eight languages.

Polyphony
Lesley Saunders

A sunset is splashing panes of gold
over the great hall and something like blue
is gathering in corners where the walls
are about to become fully themselves,
moody and mottled, polyphonies
of slab and lime, roughcast and lath
leaning into the space, *ecce carissimi*.
Lapped in dusk, we prepare to listen.

The music is dissonant, subtle, multiple,
it has nuances beyond the voices
of the faithful, it fragments the known
and familiar, it is frivolous, obscure, absurd.
It leaps and floods the air …
When, as now, there is only doctrine
and the savagery of civil strife — the saved
and the damned, the leavers and the stayers —
only torsos remain; the old corpus
of thanksgiving is meat for beasts of the field;
stony desolation and stumbling grief
are diminished to scream while indignation,
righteous wrath, ire, collapse in infantile rage.

Such a loss of abundance, such a reduction
of habitat for galliards and pavanes!
The mistress of ceremonies lights the candles:

we sit in our own shadows, falling into fugue,
souls trapped between either and or.
At our backs, behind the locked door,
stand indigo, kingfisher, turquoise, perse,
azure, jasper, smalt, violet, ultramarine,
arms raised in a *gloria*, force-fields
of heteroglossia, pageants of richness,
tall guardians against the violence of binary.

In the Hearts of Pioneers
Carl Sandburg

The following essay was adapted from Carl Sandburg's prologue to Family of Man, *a book published alongside the photography exhibit of the same name which, starting in the mid 1950s, toured all corners of the world for eight years. Edward Steichen, Sandburg's brother-in-law and director of photography at New York's Museum of Modern Art, curated the exhibit. It was as if humanity was seeing itself in the mirror for the very first time. As you read Sandburg's epiphanic prologue, imagine you're living in 1955 — five years before the first televised Olympic Games, and four decades before the first graphical web browser[1] — when photography remained a precious and rare glimpse into the lives of others around the world. This was a time when you could peer at a photograph and see the world looking back at you grand and strange and beautiful.*

—JONATHAN SIMONS

The first cry of a newborn baby in Chicago or Zamboango, in Amsterdam or Rangoon, has the same pitch and key, each saying, "I am! I have come through! I belong! I am a member of the Family."

People! flung wide and far, born into toil, struggle, blood and dreams, among lovers, eaters, drinkers, workers, loafers,

---

1 Namely Mosaic, released in 1993 and developed by NASA's National Center for Supercomputing Applications, with funding from Senator Al Gore's High Performance Computing Act of 1991.—*Ed.*

fighters, players, gamblers. Here are ironworkers, bridgemen, musicians, sandhogs, miners, builders of huts and skyscrapers, jungle hunters, landlords and the landless, the loved and the unloved, the lonely and abandoned, the brutal and the compassionate — one big family hugging close to the ball of Earth for its life and being.

Here or there you may witness a startling harmony where you say, "This will be haunting me a long time with a loveliness I hope to understand better."

In a seething of saints and sinners, winners or losers, in a womb of superstition, faith, genius, crime, sacrifice, here is the People, the one and only source of armies, navies, work-gangs, the living flowing breath of the history of nations, ever lighted by the reality or illusion of hope. Hope is a sustaining human gift.

Everywhere is love and love-making, weddings and babies from generation to generation keeping the Family of Man alive and continuing. Everywhere the sun, moon and stars, the climates and weathers, have meanings for people. Though meanings vary, we are alike in all countries and tribes in trying to read what sky, land and sea say to us. Alike and ever alike we are on all continents in the need of love, food, clothing, work, speech, worship, sleep, games, dancing, fun. From tropics to arctics humanity lives with these needs so alike, so inexorably alike.

Hands here, hands gnarled as thorn-tree roots and others soft as faded rose leaves. Hands reaching, praying and groping, hands holding tools, torches, brooms, fishnets, hands doubled in fists of flaring anger, hands moving in caress of beloved faces. The hands and feet of children playing ring-around-a-rosy — countries and languages different but the little ones alike in playing the same game.

Here are set forth babies arriving, suckling, growing into youths restless and questioning. Then as grownups they seek and hope. They mate, toil, fish, quarrel, sing, fight, pray, on all parallels and meridians having likeness. The earliest man, ages ago, had tools, weapons, cattle, as seen in his cave drawings. And like him the latest man of our day has his tools, weapons, cattle. The earliest man struggled through inexpressibly dark chaos of hunger, fear, violence, sex. A long journey it has been from that early Family of Man to the one of today which has become a still more prodigious spectacle.

Often faces speak what words can never say. Some tell of eternity and others only the latest tattlings. Faces having land and sea on them, faces honest as the morning sun flooding a clean kitchen with light, faces crooked and lost and wondering where to go this afternoon or tomorrow morning. Faces in crowds, laughing and windblown leaf faces, profiles in an instant of agony, mouths in a dumbshow mockery lacking speech, faces of music in gay song or a twist of pain, a hate ready to kill, or calm and ready-for-death faces. Some of them are worth a long look now and deep contemplation later. Faces betokening a serene blue sky or faces dark with storm winds and lashing night rain. And faces beyond forgetting, written over with faiths in men and dreams of man surpassing himself. An alphabet here and a multiplication table of living breathing human faces.

In the times to come as in the past there will be generations taking hold as though loneliness and the genius of struggle has always dwelt in the hearts of pioneers.

Excerpted from Carl Sandburg, prologue to *Family of Man* (New York: The Museum of Modern Art, 1955), pp. 4–5.

Too Many Images
Robert Frank

There are too many images, too many cameras now. We're all being watched. It gets sillier and sillier. As if all action is meaningful. Nothing is really all that special. It's just life. If all moments are recorded, then nothing is beautiful and maybe photography isn't an art anymore.

Charlie LeDuff, "Robert Frank's Unsentimental Journey," *Vanity Fair* (April 2008), p. 164.

Their Own Voices
Sherry Turkle

For children growing up, the capacity for self-reflection is the bedrock of development. Unlike time with a book, where one's mind can wander and there is no constraint on time out for self-reflection, "apps" bring children back to the task at hand. One of the things modeling clay and paints and blocks did for children was slow them down. When you watch children play with them, you see how the physicality of the materials offers a resistance that gives children time to think, to use their imaginations, to make up their own worlds. Children learn to experience this time alone as pleasurable solitude for getting to know themselves. It is in this area that I have my greatest misgiving: the screens promise that you will never have to be alone.

We can already see that so many adults are terrified to be alone. At a red light or a supermarket checkout, they panic and reach for a device. Our lives with screens seem to have left us with the need to constantly connect. Instead of being able to use time alone to think, we think only of filling the time with connection. We seem to believe that if we are connected we'll never be lonely. But in fact the truth is quite the opposite. If all we do is compulsively connect, we will be more lonely. […] It is one thing for adults to choose distraction over self-reflection. But children need to learn to hear their own voices.

The Mediation of Experience
Jerry Mander

Natural environments have largely given way to human-created environments. What we see, hear, touch, smell, feel, and understand about the world has been processed for us. Our experiences of the world can no longer be called direct, or primary. They are secondary, mediated experiences.

When we are walking in a forest, we can see and feel what the planet produces directly. Forests grow on their own without human intervention. When we see a forest, or experience it in other ways, we can count on the experience being directly between us and the planet. It is not mediated, interpreted, or altered.

On the other hand, when we live in cities, no experience is directly between us and the planet. Virtually all experience is mediated in some way. Concrete covers whatever would grow from the ground. Buildings block the natural vistas. The water we drink comes from a faucet, not from a stream or the sky. All foliage has been confined by human considerations and redesigned according to human tastes. There are no wild animals, there are no rocky terrains, there is no cycle of bloom and decline. There is not even night and day. No food grows anywhere. Most of us give little importance to this change in human experience of the world, if we notice it at all. We are so surrounded by a reconstructed world that it is difficult to grasp how astonishingly different it is from the world of only one hundred years ago, and that it bears virtually no resemblance to the world in which human beings lived for four million years before that. That this might affect the way we think, including our understanding of how our lives are connected to any nonhuman system, is rarely considered.

In fact, most of us assume that human understanding is now more thorough than before, that we know more than we ever did. This is because we have such faith in our rational, intellectual processes and the institutions we have created that we fail to observe their limits.

A Basic Problem
David Foster Wallace

I understand that there is a certain amount of hope about the Internet democratizing people. The fact of the matter is, it seems to me, if you still have a nation of people sitting in front of screens pretending, you know, interacting with images rather than each other, feeling lonely and needing more and more images, you're going to have the same basic problem: the better the images get, the more tempting it's going to be to interact with images rather than other people, and I think the emptier it's going to get.

Excerpted from an interview with David Foster Wallace by Christopher Lydon, *The Connection*, Radio Open Source (February 21, 1996), audio, 31:29.

Alone Together
Geert Lovink

While melancholy in the past was defined by separation from others, reduced contacts and reflection on oneself, today's *tristesse* plays itself out amidst busy social (media) interactions. In Sherry Turkle's phrase, we are alone together,[1] as part of the crowd—a form of loneliness that is particularly cruel, frantic and tiring.

What we see today are systems that constantly disrupt the timeless aspect of melancholy. There's no time for contemplation, or *Weltschmerz*.[2] Social reality does not allow us to retreat. Even in our deepest state of solitude we're surrounded by (online) others that babble on and on, demanding our attention. But distraction does not just take us away from the world—this is the old, if still prevalent way of framing the fatal attraction of smart phones. No, distraction does not pull us away, but instead draws us back into the social. Social reality is the magic realm where we belong. That's where the tribes gather, and that's the place to be—on top of the world. Social relations in "real life" have lost their supremacy. The idea of going back to the village mentality of the place formerly known as "real life" is daunting indeed.

---

1   Sherry Turkle, *Alone Together* (London: Basic Books, 2011).

2   "A feeling of sadness about the state of the world." *Oxford Advanced Learner's Dictionary*, 9th ed. (2015). German, formed as *Welt* (world) and *Schmerz* (pain).—*Ed.*

The Busy Man Speaks
Robert Bly

Not to the mother of solitude will I give myself
Away, not to the mother of love, nor to the mother
    of conversation,
Nor to the mother of art, nor the mother
Of tears, nor the mother of the ocean;
Not to the mother of sorrow, nor the mother
Of the downcast face, nor the mother of the suffering of death;
Not to the mother of the night full of crickets,
Nor the mother of the open fields, nor the mother of Christ.

But I will give myself to the father of righteousness, the father
Of cheerfulness, who is also the father of rocks,
Who is also the father of perfect gestures;
From the Chase National Bank
An arm of flame has come, and I am drawn
To the desert, to the parched places, to the landscape of zeros;
And I shall give myself away to the father of righteousness,
The stones of cheerfulness, the steel of money, the father
    of rocks.

Robert Bly, *The Light Around the Body* (New York: Harper & Row, 1967), p. 4.

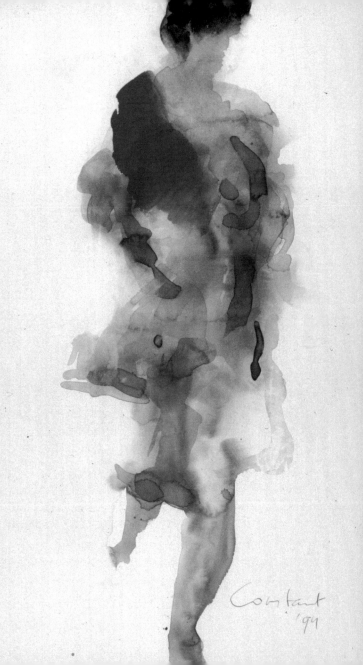

Back to the Spectacle
Kevin Fox Gotham

I n 1967, Guy Debord published his magnum opus, *The Society of the Spectacle*, which presented a stunningly original critique of consumer capitalism and our image-obsessed and image-dominated society. The short book contained no page numbers and was written in an aphoristic style with nine chapters organized into two hundred and twenty-one theses. Drawing inspiration from Henri Lefebvre and Georg Lukács, Debord argued that modern society had moved from an era dominated by the production of commodities to one dominated by the production of spectacles. Echoing the first sentence of Volume One of Karl Marx's *Capital*, Debord maintained that "[in] those societies in which modern conditions of production prevail [life] presents itself as an immense accumulation of spectacles. All that once was directly lived has become mere representation."[1] For Debord, the spectacle is neither a collection of images nor a totality that dominates the world from the top down. Rather, the spectacle is a "social relation between people that is mediated by images."[2] This social relation reflects and reinforces broader processes of separation, fragmentation,

---

1   Guy Debord, *The Society of the Spectacle*, trans. Donald Nicholson-Smith (New York: Zone Books, 1994), p. 12.

2   Ibid.

and spectacularization. Debord maintained that "separation is the alpha and the omega of the spectacle," and individuals, atomized and dissociated from one another, rediscover their unity as "consumers" within the spectacle. In this view, social life becomes "blanketed by substratum after substratum of commodities"[3] and people become spectators of their own lives, assigned to roles that subject them to a condition of chronic passivity.

In this essay, I want to emphasize the progressive side of Debord's critique of capitalism and argue that *The Society of the Spectacle* offers insights to help us dissect and interrogate the fundamental transformations that are occurring in the world economy, politics, and culture today. Furthermore, Debord's book gives us a critical dialectical perspective that can help distinguish between the progressive and emancipatory features of modern society and its oppressive and negative attributes. This understanding requires one to address the contradictions and ambiguities of modern capitalism and the ways that relations of domination and subordination are imposed from above yet can be contested and reconfigured from below.

Debord's insights from 1967 offer us a roadmap towards a progressive future. An understanding of his work compels us to situate specific forms of spectacle within particular

---

3   Ibid., p. 29.

conflicts and social relations, thereby illuminating their connection to broader social forces that constitute or constrain them. There is no monolithic spectacle that is a fully constituted objectivity or autonomously functioning entity. Rather, there is a multiplicity of different kinds of spectacles, and all forms of spectacle are products of social relationships. Spectacles are fluid, unstable, plural, and conflictual, and they display and articulate profound contradictions.

IN *THE SOCIETY OF THE SPECTACLE*, Debord developed a multifaceted conception of the spectacle as a legitimating ideology, as a process of socio-historical development (spectacularization), and as a contemporary condition. Debord theorized that the spectacle is "capital accumulated to the point where it becomes an image"[4] and represents the "historical moment at which the commodity completes its colonization of social life."[5] In the spectacle, media and consumer society supplant lived experience, the passive gaze of images overwhelms active social participation, and new forms of alienation reinforce social atomization at a more abstract level than in previous societies. For Debord, spectacularization is a process akin to the "objectification" or "thingification" of social relations and products extended

---

4 Ibid., p. 24.

5 Ibid., p. 29.

to the production and consumption of images. Thus, individuals view and experience the "image society" as an alien force, as an independent and objective reality that controls their lives by constituting them as passive spectators. For Debord, modern capitalism is about the "manufacture of an ever-growing mass of image-objects"[6] that induce "trance-like behavior"[7] and produce estrangement.[8]

Debord elaborated on two aspects of the spectacle. First, the "concentrated spectacle" is primarily associated with bureaucratic capitalism and represents institutional apparatus of contemporary capitalism governed by class domination. Second, the "diffuse spectacle" is associated with commodity abundance and represents the totalization of commodity fetishism and reification. According to Debord:

> Here each commodity considered in isolation is justified by an appeal to the grandeur of commodity production in general — a production for which the spectacle is an apologetic catalog. The claims jostling for position on the stage of the affluent economy's integrated spectacle are not always compatible, however. Similarly, different star commodities simultaneously promote conflicting approaches to

---

6 Ibid., p. 16.

7 Ibid., p. 17.

8 Ibid., p. 26.

the organization of society; thus the spectacular logic of the automobile argues for a perfect traffic flow entailing the destruction of the old city centers, whereas the spectacle of the city itself calls for these same ancient sections to be turned into museums. So the already questionable satisfaction allegedly derived from the *consumption of the whole* is adulterated from the outset because the real consumer can only get his hands on a succession of *fragments* of this commodity heaven—fragments each of which naturally lacks any of the *quality* ascribed to the whole.[9]

Debord implies that the spectacle is legitimating ideology in which a cacophony of signs, images, and entertaining motifs and symbols operate to distort reality and thereby cloak and hide the exploitative conditions of capitalism. In both the diffuse and concentrated forms, the spectacle "is no more than an image of harmony set amidst desolation and dread, at the still center of misfortune."[10]

OVER THE DECADES, SCHOLARS AND activists have debated Debord's arguments, insights, and criticisms of modern society. Many scholars have praised and criticized his book, and journalists and others have appropriated his concept of

---

9 Ibid., pp. 42–43.

10 Ibid., p. 41.

the spectacle as a heuristic device to examine the historical development of tourism, mega-events, mass entertainment, modern cinema, cities, disasters, politics, media culture, and other cultural forms. Debord's pioneering text remains in print and, though decades have passed since it was first published, MIT Press continues to advertise the book. Condemned and celebrated, *The Society of the Spectacle* is now a classic text that is remarkably and instructively archetypal as a prescient and thorough critique of modern capitalism.

John Harris's 2012 article in the *Guardian*, "Guy Debord Predicted Our Distracted Society," suggests that *The Society of the Spectacle* articulates some aspects of the twenty-first century directly, such as "so-called celebrity culture and its portrayal of lives whose freedom and dazzle suggest almost the opposite of life as most of us actually live it." [11] According to Harris,

[W]hen Debord writes about how "behind the masks of total choice, different forms of the same alienation confront each other," I now think of social media, and the white noise of most online life. All told, the book is full of sentences that describe something simple, but profound: the way that just about everything that we consume—and, if we're

---

11 John Harris, "Guy Debord Predicted Our Distracted Society," *Guardian* (US edition; March 30, 2012).

not careful, most of what we do — embodies a mixture of distraction and reinforcement that serves to reproduce the mode of society and economy that has taken the idea of the spectacle to an almost surreal extreme. Not that Debord ever used the word, but his ideas were essentially pointing to the basis of what we now know as neoliberalism.[12]

Debord's *The Society of the Spectacle* offers a prescient analysis of the ways in which processes of pacification, depoliticization, and massification both "distract" and "seduce" people using the mechanisms of leisure, consumption, and entertainment as ruled by the dictates of advertising and commodified media culture. His book offers powerful insights and is a prophecy of the dangers of the Internet age now upon us as human social life is subsumed by technology and images.

Robert Zaretsky's 2017 critical essay in *The New York Times*, "Trump and the 'Society of the Spectacle'" suggests that "perhaps more than any other twentieth-century philosophical work, [*The Society of the Spectacle*] captures the profoundly odd moment we are now living through, under the presidential reign of Donald Trump."[13] According to Zaretsky:

---

12 Ibid.

13 Robert Zaretsky, "Trump and the 'Society of the Spectacle,'" *The New York Times* (February 20, 2017).

With the presidency of Donald Trump, the Debordian analysis of modern life resonates more deeply and darkly than perhaps even its creator thought possible, anticipating, in so many ways, the frantic and fantastical, nihilistic and numbing nature of our newly installed government. In Debord's notions of "unanswerable lies," when "truth has almost everywhere ceased to exist or, at best, has been reduced to pure hypothesis," and the "outlawing of history," when knowledge of the past has been submerged under "the ceaseless circulation of information, always returning to the same list of trivialities," we find keys to the rise of trutherism as well as Trumpism.[14]

Zaretsky's insights resonate with Debord's contention that "by means of the spectacle the ruling order discourses endlessly upon itself in an uninterrupted monologue of self-praise. The spectacle is the self-portrait of power in the age of power's totalitarian rule over the conditions of existence."[15]

OVER THE DECADES, SOME READERS have interpreted the spectacle as an omnipotent force, a steamrolling juggernaut of domination that crushes opposition and makes resistance futile. Yet we know that spectacles have diverse manifestations

---

14 Ibid.

15 Debord, p. 19.

and can be sites of contestation that exude contradictory tendencies and articulate conflictual and opposing meanings of reality. Rather than obscuring and camouflaging social problems, different spectacles and spectacular imagery can articulate and display highly contradictory representations and thereby spawn resistant agendas. Different kinds of spectacles can operate as sites of struggle and articulators of political dissent, a conception that helps to explain the increasing international opposition and protest against mega events such as the Olympics. Rather than generate conformity and quiescence, we know that media coverage of disasters, wars, and other traumatic events can create discontent, political opposition, and resistance through the mobilization of labor organizations, housing and civil-rights activists, and local community organizations.

Against monolithic conceptions of spectacle and one-sided views that stress the omnipotent and negative power of spectacle, we should view spectacles as plural (rather than unitary) and see them as fraught with conflict, struggle, and contradiction. On the one hand, the ongoing circulation of images and media representations of reality blurs the lines between news and entertainment and helps nurture an entertainment-saturated politics. Here media-focused politicians, researchers, and other experts embrace spectacle as a major component of political strategy, including impression management and damage control. On the other hand, the proliferation of spectacles and imagery insinuates its own critique of everyday life.[16] That is, critique of the society of the spectacle is already contained immanently within existing conditions. Debord developed his critique of the spectacle using *détournement*, the strategy of placing a photograph, film, advertisement, or other text in a new context in order to subvert the dominant paradigm, reveal the oppressive character of consumer capitalism, and expose the reality of poverty and material suffering.[17]

One of Debord's intentions in *The Society of the Spectacle* was to highlight the seemingly all-powerful nature of the spectacle while pointing to its subversive tendencies and contradictory aspects. The dominance of wage labor, private ownership of the means of production, and the pervasiveness of the commodity form legitimize social inequalities and impede revolutionary change. Yet the impoverishment of everyday life under these social relations of capitalism can also nurture the development of revolutionary movements. That is, commodities, consumption, and entertainment carry both the seeds of their own destruction and the conditions of their own transcendence. Consumption can never satisfy because the logic of the consumable object demands the creation of new insatiable needs.

---

16 Ibid., p. 139.

17 Ibid., pp. 144–147.

In short, Debord's *Society of the Spectacle* offers acute insights to help us to understand forces that reproduce the status quo and transform society for the better. The phrase "back to the spectacle" is a call to arms. To understand the present and carve a path to a progressive future requires reading and comprehending a short book that was released in 1967. Could we be entering a period similar to that of the widespread protests of May 1968, which represent what Debord called "lived time,"[18] in which people together question the status quo and refashion life as creative agents? The rise of new information and communication technologies offers the potential to exacerbate existing power relations and inequalities and give the major corporate forces potent new tools to advance their interests. Debord suggests that it is up to people to work together to devise strategies to use existing technologies, media forms, and other imagery to promote democratization and social justice. For as new spectacles and new technologies become ever more central to every domain of everyday life, developing resistant agenda and oppositional politics becomes more and more important. Changes in the economy, political order, and community life demand a constant reconceptualization of politics and social change in the light of spectacularization; to respond to ever-changing historical conditions, it is clear that we need new forms of critical thinking.

18 Ibid., p. 105.

Eating Menus
Alan Watts

We've run into a cultural situation where we've confused the symbol with the physical reality — the money with the wealth and the menu with the dinner. We're starving and eating menus.

Alan Watts, "The Process of Life" (lecture, IBM Systems Group Seminar, 1969).

The Art of Drifting
Libero Andreotti

One of the favorite play forms engaged in by the Situationist International and its predecessor organization, the Lettrist International, was the *dérive*, the art of wandering through urban space […] The dérive's closest cultural precedents would have been the Dadaist and Surrealist excursions organized by Breton in 1925, such as the one to the church of Saint-Julien-le-Pauvre. However, Debord was careful to distinguish the dérive from such precedents, emphasizing its active character as "a mode of experimental behavior" that ultimately reached back to romanticism, the baroque, and the age of chivalry, with its tradition of the long voyage undertaken in a spirit of adventure and discovery. In Paris this kind of urban roaming was characteristic of Left Bank bohemianism, where the art of drifting was a favorite way of cultivating that feeling of being "apart together" that Huizinga described as characteristic of play.[1]

Central to the dérive was the awareness of exploring forms of life radically beyond the capitalist work ethic, as seen in the famous graffiti incitement, "Ne travaillez jamais" (Never work), made by Debord in 1953 and reproduced in the SI's journal with the caption "minimum program of the situationist movement."

---

1 Johan Huizinga, *Homo Ludens: A Study of the Play-Element in Culture* (Boston: Beacon Press, 1990), p. 12.

Spectacle of Disintegration
McKenzie Wark

I t's getting hard to wander, and yet it's become something of a mainstream art, in the writings of Will Self,
for example. But I'm encouraged by those who keep *dérive*[1]
alive at the edge between art and everyday life. But perhaps
it's an old-world pursuit, not suited for the contemporary
megalopolis. Non-Western cities might need another
practice to unlock the secrets of another city for another life.

The practice of *dérive* is supposed to lead to the theory
and practice of unitary urbanism, which would be a built
form without private property, capitalist relations of production, and the division of work and leisure. Rather than
abolishing work, the current stage of commodification
has abolished leisure. The cell phone is an instrument of
extracting value not only from labor but also nonlabor.
Everywhere you go, everything you do with it generates
data to be harvested and monetized by some corporation
or other. The world we live in is the dialectical negation
of Constant Nieuwenhuys's *New Babylon* (1956–1974), the
highpoint of Marxist-Situationist urban utopianism. In mod-
els, maps, and drawings, Constant imagined megacities for

---

1 Literally "drift" or "drifting," *la dérive* is a technique for engaging with
urban landscapes, put forward by Guy Debord in "Théorie de la Dérive," *Les
Lèvres nues*, no. 9 (November 1956).—*Ed.*

nomadic play. Only in fiction do I think you find work that dares to imagine a whole new built form at planetary scale.

Guy Debord thought the diffuse spectacle had given way to an integrated spectacle by the 1970s, which folded the secrecy and industrialized corruption of the Soviet concentrated spectacle into its Western double. Now I think we would have to conceive of a *spectacle of disintegration*, in which the spectacle's principle of the separation of being from having, and then of having from appearing, constructs a world in which even the ruling class can no longer know itself or the world it once conquered. Now it feeds on its own fragmentation and waste products.

Debord did not see May '68 as a unique event but as part of an endless cycle of irruptions of historical time into the fashion cycle of spectacular time. The historical impasse diagnosed by the Situationist International remains, even as their strategies against it pass into and are recuperated by that history. Avant-gardes are made to die in the war of time.

La Dérive
Guy Debord

Among the various situationist practices, the *dérive*[1] is a technique of swift movement through varied environments. The concept of dérive is inextricably linked to the effects of psychogeography as well as to the individual behaving in a playful and productive manner, all of which is quite different from classic notions of a journey or stroll.

In a dérive, one or more persons spend a period of time letting go of their relations, their work and leisure activities, all other usual motives for movement and action, and instead let themselves be drawn by the seductions of the terrain and the encounters they discover along the way.

Randomness, or chance, is a less important factor in this activity than one might think. From the point of view of dérive, cities have psychogeographical contours, with constant currents of energy, fixed points, as well as vortexes which strongly discourage entry into or exit from certain areas.

Dérive, in its ideal unity, includes both a letting-go and its counterpart—a mastering of psychogeographical variations through the knowledge and study of their possibilities. Regarding this last aspect, the field of ecology is limited owing to the social sphere it claims to study and

---

1 Literally: "drift" or "drifting" —*Ed.*

therefore does not offer us much in the way of psychogeographic theory.

Chombart de Lauwe, in his study *Paris et l'agglomération Parisienne,*[2] notes that "an urban neighborhood is determined not only by geographical and economic factors, but also by the image that its inhabitants and those of other neighborhoods have of it." In the same study, in order to illustrate "the narrowness of the actual Paris in which each individual lives within a geographical area whose radius is extremely small," he diagrams the movements made in the span of one year by a student living in the Sixteenth Arrondissement. Her daily routine draws a small triangle with no significant deviations, the three points of which are the School of Political Sciences, her home, and that of her piano teacher.

There is no doubt that such studies, even if they are examples of a modern poetry capable of provoking strong emotional reactions—in this case, outrage at the fact that it's even possible to live this way—offer little toward advancing the practice of dérive.

If chance plays an important role in *la dérive* this is because the methodology of psychogeographical observation is still in its infancy. This is because our reaction to unpredictability is naturally conservative and in a new setting tends to reduce

---

2   Paul-Henry Chombart de Lauwe, *Paris et l'agglomération Parisienne* (Paris: Presses Universitaires de France, 1952).

everything to habit or at least a mere alternation between a limited number of variants. Progress means breaking through fields where chance holds sway by creating new conditions more favorable to one's purpose. We can say, then, that the randomness of a dérive is fundamentally different from that of the stroll, but also that the initial psychogeographical discoveries made by a *dériveur* may tend to fixate around new habitual axes to which the subject is repeatedly drawn back.

One can dérive alone, but all indications are that the most fruitful numerical distribution consists of several small groups of two or three people who have reached the same level of awareness, since their shared impressions make it possible for them to arrive at more objective conclusions. It is also preferable for the composition of these groups to change from one dérive to another. With more than four or five participants, the experience of dérive rapidly diminishes, and in any case it is impossible for there to be more than ten or twelve people without the dérive breaking up into several concurrent dérives. The study of such subdivision is in fact of great interest, but the difficulties it entails have so far prevented it from being organized on a sufficient scale.

The average duration of a dérive is one day—considered as the time between two periods of sleep. The starting and ending times need not relate to the solar day, but it should be noted that the last hours of the night are generally unsuitable for dérive.

But these durations are merely statistical values. For one thing, a dérive rarely appears in pure form, as it's difficult for the participants to avoid being distracted an hour or two at the beginning or end of the day by banal tasks; and toward the evening fatigue tends to encourage abandonment. Most often, a dérive occurs within a deliberately fixed period of a few hours, or even fortuitously for a few brief moments; or it may last for several days without interruption. Despite the interferences imposed by sleep, some dérives of sufficient intensity have lasted three or four days, or even longer. It is true that in the case of a series of dérives stretching over a rather long period of time, it is almost impossible to determine precisely when the state of mind specific to one dérive gives way to that of another. One particular sequence of dérives was pursued without notable interruption for around two months. Such an experience gives rise to new objective conditions of behavior that lead to the disappearance of many of the old ones.

In the "possible rendezvous," the emphasis on exploration is minimal compared to behavioral disorientation. The subject is instructed to go alone to a certain place at a specified time. He is freed from the stressful obligations of an ordinary meeting since there is no one to wait for. But since this "possible rendezvous" has brought him unexpectedly to a place he may not know, he is compelled to observe his surroundings. And it may be that the same spot has been assigned as a "possible rendezvous" for someone else whose identity he has no way of knowing. Since he may never have seen this other person before, he will feel encouraged to start up conversations with various passers-by. He may meet no one, or he may meet the person who arranged the "possible rendezvous" in the first place. In any case, especially if the time and place have been well chosen, his navigation of time will take unexpected turns. One can see the infinite potential of this pastime.

Excerpted from *Guy Debord*, "Théorie de la dérive," *Les Lèvres nues*, no. 9 (November 1956), p. 6. Translation from the French by Jonathan Simons.

Homo Spectator
Donald Kuspit

Many years ago, Max Frisch said that "technology is the knack of so arranging the world that we don't have to experience it."[1] The technology of reproduction of art eliminates the necessity of experiencing it firsthand, which involves what the art historian Ananda Coomaraswamy calls *aesthetic shock*, a perceptual experience which "shakes" us to the roots of our being, and as such is the most "serious" perceptual experience possible.[2]

The art critic Roger Fry distinguishes between aesthetic experience, in which one becomes conscious of emotions and sensations as things in themselves, and ordinary experience, in which they stimulate and are associated with action, thus obscuring their inherent qualities, and implying that they have little or no meaning in themselves.[3]

For Fry it is hard to become aesthetically conscious of emotions and sensations; it requires a sort of willing suspension of belief in the world of action. The world of action's indifference to aesthetic experience, even denial and

---

1   Daniel J. Boorstin, *The Image: A Guide to Pseudo-Events in America* (New York and Evanston: Harper & Row, 1961), p. i.

2   Ananda K. Coomaraswamy, "Samvega: Aesthetic Shock," *Harvard Journal of Asiatic Studies* 7, no. 3 (February 1943), p. 174.

3   The distinction is developed in Roger Fry, *Vision and Design* (London: Chatto & Windus, 1920), pp. 1–25.

dismissal of it as inhibiting the action necessary to survive in society, does not help matters. Only by critically turning the tables on the world of action by regarding it as an illusion, or at best a necessary evil, can one see that emotions and sensations are not illusions, but uncannily real. Tuning it out, one sees the peculiar transcendence of emotions and sensations. Only then, and with the help of what Nietzsche called the *intelligent sensuality* of art, can one enter the *aesthetic state*, an "altered" state of consciousness bringing with it "an exalted feeling of *power*" or vitality, in view of Nietzsche's belief that in the aesthetic state "we infuse a transfiguration and fullness into things and poetize about them until they reflect back our fullness and joy in life."[4]

FIRSTHAND AESTHETIC EXPERIENCE IS PRECLUDED by the secondhand experience of art in reproduction. Reproduction trumps art by appropriating it wholesale — digesting it until it is a shadow of itself. Reproduction levels its sensuality and weakens its emotional effect, subverting its vitalizing evocative power, and making it seem less intelligent than it is, and with that de-aestheticizes it, that is, renders it useless as a means to the end of aesthetic experience. Paradoxical as it may seem, reproduction, which claims to serve memory,

---

4   Friedrich Nietzsche, *The Will to Power*, trans. Walter Kaufmann and R.J. Hollingdale (New York: Vintage Books, 1968), p. 421.

leads us to forget what is most memorable — experientially real — about the art by reducing it to an appearance. The real work is superseded by its cannibalization in reproduction.

WHEN AMERICAN POP ART EMERGED in the 1960s, the joke was that it looked better in reproduction than it did in reality — an idea valorized by Andy Warhol's wish to be a star so that he could meet real stars face to face and see that they didn't look as perfect as they did in their photographs. Their faces, like his, had blemishes, which made them real. But he didn't like their reality, only their glamorized appearances.

We are all members of the society of the spectacle, which is correlate with capitalist society. Warhol, who presciently called himself a business artist, was also a celebrity artist, a servant of the society of the spectacle — an artist who preferred appearance to reality, who celebrated appearance at the expense of reality, and, indeed, used it to obscure and deny reality. The society of the spectacle is a postmodern society, in that it has given up on external as well as internal reality, treating both as codified appearances. It has given up on what psychoanalysts call reality testing. Modern art grappled with both realities, dialectically teasing out their inherent aesthetics, which became its own reality. Postmodern art subsumes modern art — and reality, internal and external — by reproducing it as a cultural code: one among many, and thus of no special consequence. It is the triumph of derealization and depersonalization over reality testing and self-realization—the realization that one is a particular person, not a social robot, or, to use Winnicott's language, has a *true self*, capable of "spontaneous gesture and personalized idea." The postmodern society of the spectacle—in which art is part of the spectacle and makes a spectacle of itself—is a psychotic society.

HOMO SPECTATOR IS SOCIALLY, CULTURALLY and economically dominant, as the situationist Guy Debord argues. For him it is not clear that *Homo spectator* is *Homo sapiens*. In the society of the spectacle, we live in fantasy, not in reality, and we are unable to distinguish them. As Debord writes, "the spectacle proclaims the predominance of appearances and asserts that all human life, which is to say all social life, is mere appearance […] it is a visible negation of life […] a negation of life that has *invented a visual form for itself*. […] It turns reality on its head." Where, in an earlier capitalist stage, there was a "downgrading of *being* into *having*," the current capitalist stage "entails a generalized shift from *having* to appearing: all effective 'having' must now derive its immediate prestige and its ultimate raison d'être from appearances." The society of the spectacle relies on "technical rationality" to produce pure appearances—especially mechanical and digital reproduction, the most rationalizing technologies for producing appearances—the more spectacular the better.

Art has credibility and exists only as a marketable, "technical" appearance in the society of the spectacle—as what Debord calls an "image-object" in the service of the "dictatorial freedom of the Market,"[5] which is the ultimate spectacle and the ultimate reason for its existence and credibility. Those who can afford to own the most marketable "artistic" appearances, as well as the business artists who produce them, become part of the spectacle as marketable appearances in their own right—those image-objects called celebrities.

In the society of the spectacle, "Publicity acquires the significance of an ideology, the ideology of trade," Henri Lefebvre writes, "and it replaces what was once philosophy, ethics, religion and aesthetics. The time is past when advertising tried to condition the consumer by the repetition of slogans; today the subtle forms of publicity represent a whole attitude to life." He adds: "publicity is the poetry of Modernity, the reason and pretext for all successful displays. It takes possession of art, literature, all available signifiers and vacant signifieds."[6] Publicity is a way of "engineering consent," to use the felicitous phrase of the sociologist Wilson Bryan Key. Publicity "assaults human perception at both conscious and unconscious levels, especially the latter," making it difficult

5   Guy Debord, *The Society of the Spectacle* (New York: Zone Books, 1995), pp. 14–18 passim.

6   Henri Lefebvre, *Everyday Life in the Modern World*, trans. Sacha Rabinovitch (New York: Harper & Row, 1971), p. 107.

to "easily discriminate between fantasy and reality." It is a form of "psychological indoctrination," leading to "self-deception" and the forfeiting of individuality.[7] "The essence of ideology is to create illusions, disguise the real, and substitute something unreal for it without this substitution being apparent," Mikel Dufrenne writes. "Why combat ideology, if not to free: and free whom, if not the individual? […] Only the individual has to be freed, and precisely because he is alienated"[8]—from his self and his humanness.

WRITING ABOUT PSEUDO-EVENTS, AND BY extension *pseudo-images*—in effect pseudo-art—the historian Daniel Boorstin notes that "from their very nature [they] tend to be more interesting than spontaneous events. […] pseudo-events tend to drive all other kinds of events out of our consciousness, or at least to overshadow them. […] The experience of spontaneous events is buried by pseudo-events."[9] Pseudo-events and pseudo-art give rise to pseudo-experience—experience which is not spontaneous but simulated and "spectacular." It is socially manufactured and

---

7   Wilson Bryan Key, *The Age of Manipulation* (New York: Henry Holt, 1989), p. 4.

8   Mikel Dufrenne, "Why Go To The Movies?," in *In the Presence of the Sensuous: Essays in Aesthetics* (Atlantic Highlands, NJ: Humanities Press International, 1987), pp. 131, 133–134.

9   Boorstin, 37.

ordained experience, and thus pseudo-personal. The *false self* has false experience; as Winnicott indicates, it is incapable of "creative apperception" of reality.

A reality-deceiving pseudo-experience occurred at the Vancouver Olympics in 2010. In an article in *The New York Times,* headlined "After Skating, A Unique Olympic Event: Crying,"[10] Juliet Macur describes how crying was turned into spectacle through being stripped of its subjective meaning and spontaneity and objectified as a programmed marketable appearance. Crying was commodified as a pseudo-event by the television media that publicized it and thereby used to stimulate the sales of the products they advertise in the intervals between their reporting of Olympic events. Media analysts have shown that more visual spacetime is given to the money-making advertising agenda than to the "live" sporting event whose every detail they claim to be covering. The event becomes an entertaining adjunct to the advertising, not vice versa. It is derealized and depersonalized, while the technology of advertising "realizes" and personalizes the product. The event is used to market the product and becomes a way to publicize it—part of the sales pitch—completing its derealization and depersonalization, that is, its pseudoification and psychoticizing. As Brett and Michael Yormark

---

10 Juliet Macur, "After Skating, a Unique Olympic Event: Crying," *The New York Times* (February 21, 2010), p. 43.

say—they are the directors of the huge BankAtlantic Sports Center in Broward County, Florida[11]—"teams are merely the 'show' for drawing in an audience of consumers."[12]

POSTMODERN ART EVENTS ARE NOT much different than postmodern sporting events. Indeed, the spectators—fans—of both become part of the spectacle, a point made transparently clear by Yves Klein's organization of an art opening—certainly a pseudo-event—in which the only "works" on display were the invited audience, who were only too happy to exhibit themselves, and who, in their own way, were for sale, all the more so because by becoming part of the spectacle of art they became marketable as celebrities.

As Boorstin writes, "the hero was distinguished by his achievement; the celebrity by his image or trademark. The hero created himself; the celebrity is created by the media"—created by dissemination as a media reproduction, one might say. "The hero was a big man; the celebrity is a big name." Does Klein's exhibition of the spectator make him a hero of art, a big man, or an art celebrity, a big name? Warhol seems to have been a small man inflated by media

---

11 Built in 1998, the BankAtlantic Sports Center, now the BB&T Center, was mostly publicly financed at a cost of 185 million dollars and seats 25,000 spectators.—*Ed.*

12 Johnnie L. Roberts, "Sports Biz's Double Play," *Newsweek* (December 8, 2007), p. 53.

publicity and his use of the media in his postmodern art into a big name.

With postmodernism, the psychotically reified false self comes into its own, just as art becomes a psychotic spectacle—not simply a theater of the absurd, but beyond absurdity, for absurdity has its own reality, while the postmodern theater that is the spectacle makes no pretense of addressing reality, offering instead psychotic entertainment. There is not much difference in principle between the dancing mannequins of the Radio City chorus line and the static mannequins in a Vanessa Beecroft installation, however costumed the former and naked the latter. They are both glamorized robots, derealized and depersonalized—psychoticized and reified—human beings, more particularly, theatrical appearances.

TODAY COMMODIFICATION AND REPRODUCTION constitute the only path to immortality—the uniqueness that is unreproducible and thus transcendent. There will be neither works of art nor commodities in the future—which may be here already—but aestheticized commodities—commodities that represent the entertaining *world beyond*, to refer to Debord's term, and as such are eternally elite. Marx called religion the opium of the masses; aesthetically entertaining commodities are the opium of the capitalist elite. What today we continue to call a work of art is simply a subclass of entertaining aestheticized commodity. An aestheticized commodity—which is what capitalist society would like everything to become, whether something found in nature or made by human effort—makes the old distinctions between artworld and lifeworld, workworld and consumer world obsolete. Surplus value is built into every commodity by aestheticizing it—infusing it with the intelligent sensuality Nietzsche attributed to art, thus giving it the aura of art, making it *an* experience. The more aesthetically elite the commodity, the more it becomes a unique "experience."

IF CONCEPT IS MORE IMPORTANT than the material which is used to illustrate it, if it is used at all, then any material can have "the status of art conferred" upon it, which are the words Breton used to justify Marcel Duchamp's readymades.[13] All this means is that art has become a label that can be pinned on any old donkey. The label *art* is the tail that wags it so that it is seen in a new way, without being new. The label gives the found object surplus value—marketing something as new always gives it surplus value—as though to compensate for its loss of use value. "Art" serves as the object's Emperor's New Clothes, until some clear-eyed

---

13 "Readymades" were found objects which the artist Marcel Duchamp (1887–1968) found and presented as art.

skeptic points out that the object is naked—just another object, assisted into becoming "art" by so-called theory.

Since Duchamp, theory serves as compensation for artistic and aesthetic inadequacy, not to say failure. Art must conform to theory to be convincing and taken seriously, suggesting that, because it is dependent on theory for credibility, it is not convincing in itself and is pseudo-serious. More pointedly, seeing through its theoretical pretensions — its conceptual clothing — one sees that it is another commodity, and a fraudulent one at that, for it has no use value—that is, experiential value—however high its exchange value. The theorization of art completes its commodification. Today any found object can be theorized into art, and with that commodified, even as every commodity is an art object in theory.

Conferring the status of art on something is pseudo-creative. It makes something appear to be art by designating it art, which is not much of a creative act, if it can be called one at all. Conceptualizing something as art is not the same as creatively working to make art — working some subject matter imaginatively through to master it emotionally and intellectually, to use the psychoanalytic idea of *working through* — unless conceptual deception is creative. Nonetheless, it is the way a pseudo-artist becomes a pseudo-aristocrat — a celebrity, a fixture in the society of the spectacle. The entertaining celebrity is a capitalist robot in a merchandizing spectacle. It is a society in which the art spectacle plays a crucial role, for it shows how easy it is to turn realities into appearances and persons into impersonators, not to say imposters. Wearing the royal robes of celebrity tends to be dehumanizing in that it makes the celebrity forget that he is all too human. Or one becomes a readymade human being, and thus no longer has to work at being human.

CLEARLY MASS REPRODUCTION AND CORPORATE capitalism work in strange, miraculous, dialectically slick ways, indicating their absolute power over consciousness. They have the magical power to create souvenirs of an experience we never had and no longer need as long as we have the spectacle. The spectacle is wish fulfillment at its most ironically consummate. Capitalism understands the deep human need to believe and trust, and brilliantly manipulates it by giving us faith in a make-believe aesthetic world populated by commodities — appearances of a reality that never existed — signaling there is nothing left to believe in and trust.

"By slaying the subject, reality itself becomes lifeless," Adorno said,[14] that is, merely appearance, as Debord would say. For Adorno the social result is pervasive indifference, the

---

14 Theodor W. Adorno, *Aesthetic Theory*, trans. Christian Lenhardt (London: Routledge & Kegan Paul, 1984), p. 45.

final manifestation of alienation and dehumanization. But the capitalist spectacle, however life-negating as Debord argued, and reifying as Adorno said of the culture industry that produces it, is constructed of appearances, and if the spectacle can convince us that appearance is reality, suggesting that popularity and reality are correlate — more pointedly, that reality is always and only what is popular, then the spectacle, despite its reifying effect, may have a de-reifying effect on life. Capitalism, after all, may have surplus experiential value and make an unconscious subjective and existential difference, thus redeeming itself and the spectacular society it constructs, not to say the spectacle it makes of itself. The dominant Zeitgeist is Capitalism — it defines and drives our times — suggesting that there must be Geist in it, if only in the perverse form of the spectacle and the reproductive technology that makes it seem timeless.

Warhol's Bleak Prophecy
Stephen Metcalf

Warhol's great advance was collapsing any distinction between commercial and noncommercial modes of experience. Maybe it's never been easier to make the case for his powers of influence because his afterlife has paralleled the rise of neoliberalism — the attempt to turn over all human activity, no matter how sacred, to the marketplace. Neoliberalism is simply Warholism as a theory of governance.

One difference between Warhol and Duchamp, or the Dadaists, or any of his predecessors in the nugatory arts, is that they did not have a free market to insinuate their visionary cynicism into everything we do and are. Blame neoliberalism, Instagram, the Kardashians, whatever — the habits of self-commodification that Warhol is regarded as having pioneered have gone general.

Despite its subtle and not-so-subtle ravishments, a Warhol canvas is expressively vacant. "There's no place for our spiritual eye to penetrate it," the art historian Neil Printz has said of the work. "We're just thrown back on the surface." That's true, though the effect is more dreadful than that. What made Warhol so perishingly cold was the implication that the "spiritual eye" never existed in the first place. Warhol, one observer put it, "wanted to be Greta Garbo, he wanted to be Marilyn Monroe," and to better convert himself into an icon, he withdrew behind an affect as lifeless as one of his Marilyn paintings. The deadpan rigmarole was total. It functioned as an anti-elegy. It said that nothing was lost, that nothing of depth or value had been surrendered to the image.

Warhol, a disciplined and hard worker, pretended he did nothing, and the idea that you could be famous for being famous drew to him some badly weakened souls. The Factory, curiously, let in all the pandemonium of the '60s, but none of its idealism. When the dancer Freddie Herko, a Factory regular, became the first of its many casualties, dancing out a friend's upper-floor window while high on speed in 1964, Warhol—who'd moved on from painting to moviemaking—said: "Gee, isn't it too bad we weren't there to shoot it."

Cold and mute and static—that is Pop art. Making you feel complicit in the coldness, the muteness, the stasis? That is Warhol. He impresses the viewer only insofar as the viewer's defenses against him are weak. His greatness has always lain in our failing. The less we push back on the idea that prurience and detritus represent the sum of it, the greater his powers of divination seem. The Warholian insinuation creeps out beyond the canvas, beyond the persona, to speak to the condition of all art, maybe all modernity, and with a retroactive power that rewrites everything that came before it. An inner life, a sense of vocation, a distrust of fame and a special loathing for speculative fortunes, a personal relationship with God (or nature) that the image may partake in but never supplant—Warholism negates it all. No wonder he has never been bigger.

In turning back the clock on the whingey, fatigue-exuding zombie—the Warhol played by David Bowie, who knew him personally, in the film *Basquiat*—maybe we will recover something of our own tender selves. Warhol must have known we'd go there. In black-and-white footage from the Factory days, one of his superstars makes the case for Warhol as a kind of saint. "He sees God wherever he looks," she says, "and in whoever he looks at. So that's why they call it art … just done, um, with a touch of divinity." I will give Warhol the last word. He pulls in his cupid-bow lips to better push it out. With a tiny, airless pop, all he says is: "Fudge."

Natural Beauty
Byung-Chul Han

Natural beauty is opposed to digital beauty. In digital beauty the negativity of the *other* is entirely removed. It is therefore perfectly *smooth*. It is not meant to contain any *tear*. Its signature is pleasure without any negativity, namely the *Like*. Digital beauty forms a *smooth space of the same*, which does not permit anything alien, any *alterity*, to enter. The pure *inside* without any exteriority is the mode in which it appears. It turns even nature into a *window* of itself. Thanks to the total digitalization of being, there is a total subjectivizing, an *absolute subjectivity* under which the human being only encounters itself.

The temporality of natural beauty is the *already of the not-yet*. It appears on the utopian horizon of what is *coming*. The temporality of digital beauty, by contrast, is the immediate present without a *future*, even without *history*. It *simply is present*, while a distance is inherent to natural beauty: the latter "veils itself at the moment of greatest proximity."[1] Its auratic distance removes it from any kind of consumption: "As indeterminate, as antithetical to definitions, natural beauty is indefinable, and in this it is related to music, [...] just as in music what is beautiful flashes up in nature only to

1 Theodor W. Adorno, *Aesthetic Theory*, trans. Robert Hullot-Kentor (London: Continuum, 1997).

disappear in the instant one tries to grasp it." Natural beauty and artistic beauty are not opposed to each other. Rather, art imitates "natural beauty as such"—"what is unutterable in the language of nature." In doing so, it saves it. Artistic beauty is the "afterimage of the silence that is the single medium through which nature speaks."

Natural beauty turns out to be "the trace of the non-identical in things under the spell of universal identity." Digital beauty banishes any negativity of the non-identical. It only permits consumable, usable *differences*. *Alterity* gives way to *diversity*. The digital world, in a manner of speaking, is a world that the humans have coated over with their own retina. This humanly *networked* world produces a permanent self-mirroring. The closer the net is woven, the more thoroughly the world shields itself against the other, the outside. The digital retina turns the world into a screen-and-control monitor. Inside this autoerotic visual space, in this *digital inwardness*, there can be no sense of wonder. The only thing human beings still like is themselves.

Byung-Chul Han, *Saving Beauty*, trans. Daniel Steuer (Cambridge: Polity Press, 2018), pp. 25–26. All quotations in this piece are from Theodor W. Adorno, *Aesthetic Theory*, trans. Robert Hullot-Kentor (London: Continuum, 1997).

The Floor
Russell Edson

For Charles Simic

The floor is something we must fight against. Whilst seemingly mere platform for the human stance, it is that place that men fall to.

I am not dizzy. I stand as a tower, a lighthouse; the pale ray of my sentiency flowing from my face.

But should I go dizzy I crash down into the floor; my face into the floor, my attention bleeding into the cracks of the floor.

Dear horizontal place, I do not wish to be a rug. Do not pull at the difficult head, this teetering bulb of dread and dream …

Solitude and the Creative Life
Fenton Johnson

G o to any bookstore and you'll find shelves of books written about living in a relationship—how to find a relationship, how to hold one together once it's found, how to survive its falling apart, how to find one again. Churches offer classes, preachers preach, teachers teach, therapists counsel about how to get and stay coupled.

Then try looking for lessons in solitude. You will search for a long while, even though more and more of us are living alone, whether by choice or circumstance. Today more than a quarter of U.S. households have only one resident. Other developed nations report higher figures, as high as sixty percent in parts of Scandinavia. This isn't just a Western phenomenon: China and India both show rapidly expanding percentages of people living solo.

If you return to that hypothetical bookstore, you will find that a remarkable number of the classics on its shelves were written by solitary travelers. Evidently some wisdom is available to these millions of people who are seeking, or at least experiencing, solitude.

After more than twenty years of living alone, I launched an investigation of how these authors lived out solitude in a world that seems so exclusively to celebrate coupling up, that sees bachelor- or spinsterhood as tragic. In search of a rich perspective on the solitary life, I embarked on a tour of the work, lives, and homes of solitary writers and artists. I hoped to learn what they had to teach about the dignity and challenge of such living amid a barrage of technology that is hell-bent on ensuring that we are never, ever alone.

I am not writing about what demographers call *singles* — a word that means nothing outside the context of marriage. Nor am I writing about hermits. I am writing, rather, about *solitaries,* to use the term favored by the Trappist monk and mystic Thomas Merton. The call to solitude is universal. It requires no cloister walls and no administrative bureaucracy, only the commitment to sit down and still ourselves to our particular aloneness. I want to consider solitary people and those who seek solitude as essential threads in the human weave — "figures in the carpet," to adapt the title of a Henry James short story narrated by just such a person — spinsters and bachelors without whom the social fabric would be threadbare, impoverished. I want to rethink our understanding of solitude and of solitaries, of those who live alone or who dedicate much of their time to being alone.

Though late in life James warned a young writer about the crushing isolation of writing, he was notably gregarious, as was Walt Whitman. Emily Dickinson, our high priestess of solitude, lived with her family and participated in its social events, which included hosting the leading literary and political figures of her time. Some of the solitaries who interest me married (e.g. Paul Cézanne, Zora Neale Hurston, Rainer

Maria Rilke), though the marriages were often stormy (as in Cézanne's case) or brief (Hurston) or carried on at a distance (Rilke). While their biographies often suggest a lifetime of living alone (e.g. Henry James, Henry David Thoreau), more emphatically and more profoundly I see their solitude enacted in their work, which is their gift to us, their spiritual children. In reading or looking at or listening to their writing or art or music, I recognized that they and I had something in common—a deep core of aloneness, a desire to define, explore, and complete the self by turning inward rather than looking outward.

In 1990, after learning of my partner's death, a dear friend wrote, "The suffering at such times can be great, I know. But it is somehow comforting to learn, even through suffering, how large and powerful love is." I would modify his eloquent condolence by substituting "especially" for "even"—for how else do we learn the dimensions and power of love except through suffering? Living amid the culture's obsession with erotic passion, a solitary exists—let us not deny it—in a state of continual suffering, which is to say, in a continual opening to the possibility and grandeur of love.

TO DEFINE A SOLITARY AS someone who is not married—to define solitude as the absence of coupling—is like defining silence as the absence of noise. Solitude and silence are positive gestures. This is why Buddhists say that we can learn what we need to know by sitting on a cushion. This is why I say that you can learn what you need to know from the silent, solitary discipline of writing, the discipline of art. This is why I say that solitaries possess the key to saving us from ourselves.

Among my ideal solitaries: Siddhāratha Gautama sitting under the bodhi tree; Moses on the mountain, demanding a name from the voice in the wind; Jacob wrestling with his angel; Judith with the blade of her sword raised over the head of the sleeping Holofernes; John baptizing in the waters of the Jordan; Jesus fasting in the wilderness for forty days and forty nights, Jesus in his agony in the garden, Jesus in his agony on the cross; the Magdalen among the watching women, the Magdalen discovering the empty tomb; Matsuo Bashō setting out on his journey to the deep north. For exemplars closer to our time, I study the lives and work of Dietrich Bonhoeffer, Paul Cézanne, Hart Crane, Dorothy Day, Emily Dickinson, Marsden Hartley, Langston Hughes, Zora Neale Hurston, Henry James, Thomas Merton, Flannery O'Connor, Eudora Welty.

As I spent time studying these writers and artists, I began to experience them speaking to me, haunting me, appearing as visions, their voices urging me onward in my quest to see their solitude not as tragedy or bad luck but as an integral and necessary aspect of who they were. In their works and stories they spoke as witnesses in a great cloud around me:

Thoreau ("The man who goes alone can start today; but he who travels with another must wait till that other is ready, and it may be a long time before they get off"); Louisa May Alcott ("I'd rather be a free spinster and paddle my own canoe"); Marianne Moore ("I should like to be alone").

I am not interested in the possibility that solitaries might lead more carefree lives. My ideal solitary carries not less but more responsibility toward the self and the universe than those who couple. The solitary hasn't the luxury of what Ross Douthat, a columnist for *The New York Times,* recently called "deep familial selfishness." Solitude imposes on its practitioners a choice between emotional atrophy and openness to the world, with all the reward and heartbreak that generosity implies.

But now we come to the nub of the question, the hub of the turning wheel of the teachings: What figure does the solitary cut in the human tapestry? What is the usefulness of sitting alone at one's desk and writing, especially writing those vast seas of pages that will see only the recycling bin? What is the usefulness of meditation, or of prayer? What is the usefulness of the solitary?

"THE FREE MAN BELIEVES IN destiny and believes that it has need of him," wrote Martin Buber, the great Jewish philosopher. "Destiny," the spinster poet Marianne Moore repeated. "Not *fate*."

What is this distinction Moore takes such care to draw between destiny and fate? Fate suggests submission to the circumstances of life; destiny suggests active engagement. The former implies some all-powerful force or figure to whose will we must submit. The latter implies that each of us is a manifestation of one of the infinite aspects of creation, whose fullest expression depends in some small but necessary way on our day-to-day, moment-to-moment decisions. We are caught—trapped, some might say—in the web of fate, but we are each just as surely among its multitude of spinners. In our spinning lies our hope; in our spinning lies our destiny. In this way, just as marriages or partnerships are not given but made, solitaries can consciously embrace and inhabit their solitude.

The solitaries who achieved destinies worthy of the name formed and cultivated special relationships with the great silence, the great Alone. I sense that relationship in their work. I read it in their poetry, in their stories, in their novels; I see it in their painting; I hear it in their music. Again and again the bachelor Giorgio Morandi painted vessels that float outside time and space in a world without surface or shadow, portraits of infinity. Erik Satie composed music in which the silences are as important as the notes. Of the solitary music teacher she created in her story "June Recital," Eudora Welty, a spinster, later wrote:

Miss Eckhart came from me. There wasn't any resemblance in her outward identity … . What counts is only what lies at the solitary core … . What I have put into her is my passion for my own life work, my own art. Exposing yourself to risk is a truth Miss Eckhart and I had in common. What animates me and possesses me is what drives Miss Eckhart, the love of her art and the love of giving it, the desire to give it until there is no more left.

In Welty's story "Music from Spain," Eugene, the protagonist, first imagines that a touring Spanish guitarist he has met has a lover in every port, only to decide that "it was more probable that the artist remained alone at night, aware of being too hard to please — and practicing on his guitar."

I do not wish to say that being solitary is superior or inferior to being coupled, nor that the full experience of solitude requires living alone, though doing so may create a greater silence in which to hear an inner voice. Bachelorhood is a legitimate vocation. Spinsterhood is a calling, a destiny. I am seeking to understand more deeply this peculiar vocation, to which, evidently, I have been called, and which, evidently, more and more people are undertaking.

AFTER MORE THAN A DECADE of assembling evidence of his monastic order's history of supporting hermits, Merton received permission to retreat from the communal life of the monastery to a hermitage on Gethsemani's grounds. His porch offered a view across meadows rolling toward Muldraugh's Hill, the blue horizon of my childhood, which extends in a hundred-plus-mile arc around the Kentucky Bluegrass.

Merton's hermitage still overlooks those meadows. But the monks now report their silent retreatants' delight at the installation of the tallest cell tower I've seen, the red light at its top a continual winking feature of the view from Merton's porch.

The multiplication of our society's demons has been accompanied by a ratcheting up of the sources and volume of its background noise. What is the point of the chatter and diversions of our lives, except to keep the demons at bay? Meanwhile, we are creating demons faster than we can create noise to drown them out—environmental devastation, global warming, the growing gap between the rich and the poor, uncontrolled population growth, uncontrolled consumption held up by the media as the glittering purpose of life.

The appropriate response is not more noise. The appropriate response is more silence.

To choose to be alone is to bait the trap, to create a space the demons cannot resist entering. And that's the good news: the demons that enter can be named, written about, and tamed through the miracle of the healing word, the miracle of art, the miracle of silence.

"I find ecstasy in living—the mere sense of living is joy enough," Dickinson wrote. That joy, that ecstasy that she describes—I know it is not limited to celibates or solitaries, but I also know it shows itself to us in particular ways that are denied those who are coupled. Visions appear to the solitary prophet. Revelations arrive in silence and solitude. Emily Dickinson at her sunny, south-facing window, surveying the church she declined to attend, Buddha under the bodhi tree, Moses on the mountain, Jesus in the desert, Julian of Norwich in her cell, Jane Austen taking notes on the edges of the society she so vividly portrayed, Vincent van Gogh at his canvas, Zora Neale Hurston experiencing extraordinary visions while walking home alone—for these people, solitude was a vehicle for the imagination.

Only in solitude could these solitaries fulfill their destinies—become not partial but *whole*—teachers for you and me, teachers for and of the universe. Like Jesus, bachelor for the ages, they keep ever before us the ideal toward which we may strive. They raise the bar of what it means to be alive. By striving toward their ideal we become better than we thought ourselves capable of being.

LET US IMAGINE, AS BOTH William James and Thomas Merton proposed, a secular monasticism—a *conversatio morum,* a great conversion of manners, in the terminology of the monastic vows—an integration of mystery into our daily lives, an opulent asceticism. Walt Whitman and Emily Dickinson will be our entirely worthy Peter and Paul, and we will have as the crowning achievement of the American experiment an authentically American destiny. In this conception of the world, we celebrate friendship as the queen of virtues, and recognize it as the foundation for all worthy human connection, including marriage.

If this sounds utopian, I offer Zoketsu Norman Fischer's Everyday Zen, whose goal is to integrate Zen meditation and principles—which is to say, monastic principles—into daily life. I offer the oblate movement—even as the numbers decline in Christian religious orders, the number of people who have taken vows of allegiance to their principles is growing. I offer the growing integration of the concept of sustainability into our everyday choices. I offer the growing understanding within science and medicine of the interrelatedness of all disciplines, of all life, including that other version of life we call death.

I point to the great failure of the left—as played out in the presidency of Barack Obama, who was inaugurated with such hope—to provide a vision sufficiently grand to counter the call to unrestrained consumption that is trotted before us at every hour of every day in every popular medium. My vision is no more fantastic than colonies on Mars, solar grids in space, heat transfer from the oceans, impregnable vaults for nuclear waste, carbon-dioxide storage under the

Great Plains, or any of hundreds of proposals our politicians and research institutions and media take seriously. It requires no trillion-dollar investment in technology, which history teaches us will inevitably generate problems equal to or greater than those they solve.

Merton writes of solitaries that we are "a mute witness, a secret and even invisible expression of love which takes the form of [our] own option for solitude in preference to the acceptance of social fictions." And what love are we solitaries mute witnesses to? The omnipresence of great aloneness, the infinite possibilities of no duality, no separation between you and me, between the speaker and the spoken to, the dancer and his dance, the writer and her reader, the people and our earth.

Integrity
Thomas Merton

Many poets are not poets for the same reason that many religious men are not saints: they never succeed in being themselves. They never become the man or artist who is called for by all the circumstances of their individual lives. They waste their years in vain efforts to be some other poet, some other saint. They wear out their minds and bodies in a hopeless endeavor to have somebody else's experiences or write somebody else's poems. They want quick success and they are in such haste to get it that they cannot take time to be true to themselves.

Thomas Merton, *Seeds of Contemplation* (Norfolk, CT: New Directions, 1949), p. 75.

On the Deck of the World
Henry David Thoreau

It seemed to me that I had several more lives to live, and could not spare any more time for that one. It is remarkable how easily and insensibly we fall into a particular route, and make a beaten track for ourselves. I had not lived there a week before my feet wore a path from my door to the pond-side; and though it is five or six years since I trod it, it is still quite distinct. It is true, I fear, that others may have fallen into it, and so helped to keep it open. The surface of the earth is soft and impressible by the feet of men; and so with the paths which the mind travels. How worn and dusty, then, must be the highways of the world, how deep the ruts of tradition and conformity! I did not wish to take a cabin passage, but rather to go before the mast and on the deck of the world, for there I could best see the moonlight amid the mountains. I do not wish to go below now.

I learned this, at least, by my experiment: that if one advances confidently in the direction of his dreams, and endeavors to live the life which he has imagined, he will meet with a success unexpected in common hours. He will put some things behind, will pass an invisible boundary; new, universal, and more liberal laws will begin to establish themselves around and within him; or the old laws be expanded, and interpreted in his favor in a more liberal sense, and he will live with the license of a higher order of beings.

In proportion as he simplifies his life, the laws of the universe will appear less complex, and solitude will not be solitude, nor poverty poverty, nor weakness weakness. If you have built castles in the air, your work need not be lost; that is where they should be. Now put the foundations under them.

Excerpted from Henry David Thoreau, "Conclusion," in *Walden; or, Life in the Woods* (Boston: Ticknor and Fields, 1854), pp. 345–346.

Homelessness
Leonard Cohen

It's always an effort to feel at home. It's not something that is given to any man. It's a reward for a certain kind of effort, a certain kind of activity. If you can dissolve your own sense of alienation, your own sense of separateness, then you can feel at home in most places. If you can't, it doesn't matter where you are — you're not going to be at home. So that really is the challenge that every man faces, to dissolve the barriers between him and the rest of the world so that he *can* feel at home. Especially for someone as screwed up as I am, the effort is always to dissolve the barriers that inhibit this feeling of being at home. In other words, we mostly suffer from a feeling of homelessness. We mostly suffer from a feeling of not being at home in our skins and our hearts and our minds. So the question of being at home *is* the paramount question for people, whether they can locate those factors — those characteristics, those mindsets — that enable them to feel secure in themselves wherever they are.

Excerpted and transcribed from an audio recording of an interview with Leonard Cohen of unknown origin.

The Dream Bird
Sergio Benvenuto

Starting in the eighteenth century, the idea that human life is nothing but an escape from boredom gains affirmation. This thesis implies that boredom is a very useful sentiment. Indeed, young children already display it; as soon as they come into contact with the external world, they begin to look for interesting stimuli, objects in motion, and so on. And if no stimulus captures them, they cry. Often we wonder why they are crying, but it is quite clear that they are bored, that they are demanding something that will amuse them. At times, even cats and dogs clearly cry because they are bored; they would like to play.

This idea of life as a struggle against boredom takes root in the Utilitarianism of Jeremy Bentham and James Mill, for whom the essence of human beings consists in escaping pain. Avoidance of pain, however, is not enough; in fact, its absence becomes boring, and, in turn, causes further pain. The essence of humans, therefore, is not only to escape pain but also to find pleasure, indeed always to seek new enjoyments. Yet boredom is a zero-degree pain: once we have tried all pleasures in the effort to fend it off, boredom is again ready to set in. Being bored thus signals that we cannot stop desiring, that we feel compelled to desire because only desire gives us life. From here we see the development of a positive concept of boredom as a sentiment that allows us to hunt for new desires and dislodges us from a sort of satisfied indolence. Walter Benjamin adopts this idea of boredom as the whip of creativity: "Boredom is the dream bird that hatches the egg of experience. A rustling in the leaves drives him away. His nesting places—the activities that are intimately associated with boredom—are already extinct in the cities and are declining in the country as well."[1] Benjamin laments the fragility of boredom, its transience, because only boredom can give birth to the chick that is the creative idea that starts from experience.

1   Walter Benjamin, "The Storyteller," in *Illuminations: Essays and Reflections*, trans. H. Zohn (New York: Schocken Books, 1936), p. 91.

Sergio Benvenuto, "The Silent Fog," *American Imago* 75, no. 1 (Spring 2018), pp. 18–19.

Poetry
A Third Grader

Poetry is an egg with a horse inside.

The Way the Day Starts
Penelope Hewlett

He rises with the sun,
to sit and watch the light grow
or close his eyes and let the silence fill him,
as mist on the common fills the quiet spaces
between leaf and tree.

With his back to the night-cold wall of his home
he takes the light and sews it into prayer,
weaving a wordless web of each day's creation
back into being.

This is how he learns what the leaf thinks,
how the ground feels when we walk on it,
the way the sun burns its thoughts into the atmosphere.

This is how he lets the world turn on its axis within him,
knows how to place each foot lightly on the earth,
feels the blood in his veins understand
the sap of trees, the tears of children.

This is the way the day starts,
waiting for light to soak into his skin,
like a door inside himself, opening.

How to Keep and Feed a Muse
Ray Bradbury

I t isn't easy. Nobody has ever done it consistently. Those who try hardest scare it off into the woods. Those who turn their backs and saunter along, whistling softly between their teeth, hear it treading quietly behind them, lured by a carefully acquired disdain. We are of course speaking of *the muse*. The term has fallen out of the language in our time. More often than not when we hear it now we smile and summon up images of some fragile Greek goddess, dressed in ferns, harp in hand, stroking the brow of your perspiring scribe. The muse, then, is that most terrified of all the virgins. She starts if she hears a sound, pales if you ask her questions, spins and vanishes if you disturb her dress.

What ails her? you ask. Why does she flinch at the stare? Where does she come from and where go? How can we get her to visit for longer periods of time? What temperature pleasures her? Does she like loud voices, or soft? Where do you buy food for her, and of what quality and quantity, and what hours for dining?

It is my contention that in order to keep a muse, you must first offer food. How you can feed something that isn't yet there is a little hard to explain. Through a lifetime, by ingesting food and water, we build cells, we grow, we become larger and more substantial. That which was not, *is*. The process is undetectable. It can be viewed only at intervals along the way. We know it is happening, but we don't know quite how or why.

Similarly, in a lifetime, we stuff ourselves with sounds, sights, smells, tastes, and textures of people, animals, landscapes, events, large and small. We stuff ourselves with these impressions and experiences and our reaction to them. Into our subconscious go not only factual data but reactive data, our movement toward or away from the sensed events.

These are the stuffs, the foods, on which the muse grows. This is the storehouse, the file, to which we must return every waking hour to check reality against memory, and in sleep to check memory against memory, which means ghost against ghost, in order to exorcise them, if necessary.

What is the subconscious to every other man, in its creative aspect becomes, for writers, the muse. They are two names for one thing. But no matter what we call it, here is the core of the individual we pretend to extol, to whom we build shrines and hold lip services in our democratic society. Here is the stuff of originality. For it is in the totality of experience reckoned with, filed, and forgotten, that each man is truly different from all others in the world. For no man sees the same events in the same order, in his life. One man sees death younger than another, one man knows love more quickly than another.

We know how fresh and original is each man, even the slowest and dullest. If we come at him right, talk him along, and give him his head, and at last say, What do you want? (or if the man is very old, What *did* you want?) every man will speak his dream. And when a man talks from his heart, in his moment of truth, he speaks poetry.

We can learn from every man or woman or child around us when, touched and moved, they tell of something they loved or hated this day, yesterday, or some other day long past. At a given moment, the fuse, after sputtering wetly, flares, and the fireworks begin. Oh, it's limping crude hard work for many, with language in their way. But I have heard farmers tell about their very first wheat crop on their first farm after moving from another state, and if it wasn't Robert Frost talking, it was his cousin, five times removed. I have heard locomotive engineers talk about America in the tones of Thomas Wolfe who rode our country with his style as they ride it in their steel. I have heard mothers tell of the long night with their firstborn when they were afraid that they and the baby might die. And I have heard my grandmother speak of her first ball when she was seventeen. And they were all, when their souls grew warm, poets.

When people ask me where I get my ideas, I laugh. How strange—we're so busy looking out, to find ways and means, we forget to look *in*.

The muse, to belabor the point then, is there, a fantastic storehouse, our complete being. All that is most original lies waiting for us to summon it forth. And yet we know it is not as easy as that. We know how fragile is the pattern woven by our fathers or uncles or friends, who can have their moment destroyed by a wrong word, a slammed door, or a passing fire-wagon. So, too, embarrassment, self-consciousness, remembered criticisms, can stifle the average person so that less and less in his lifetime can he open himself out.

Let's say that each of us has fed himself on life, first, and later, on books and magazines. The difference is that one set of events happened to us, and the other was forced feeding.

If we are going to diet our subconscious, how prepare the menu? Well, we might start our list like this:

Read poetry every day of your life. Poetry is good because it flexes muscles you don't use often enough. Poetry expands the senses and keeps them in prime condition. It keeps you aware of your nose, your eye, your ear, your tongue, your hand. And, above all, poetry is compacted metaphor or simile. Such metaphors, like Japanese paper flowers, may expand outward into gigantic shapes.

What poetry? Any poetry that makes your hair stand up along your arms. Don't force yourself too hard. Take it easy. Over the years you may catch up to, move even with, and pass T. S. Eliot on your way to other pastures. You say you don't understand Dylan Thomas? Yes, but your ganglion does, and your secret wits, and all your unborn children. Read him, as you can read a horse with your eyes, set free and charging over an endless green meadow on a windy day.

What else fits in our diet? Books of essays. Here again, pick and choose, amble along the centuries. You'll have much to pick over from the days before the essay became less popular. You can never tell when you might want to know the finer points of being a pedestrian, keeping bees, carving headstones, or rolling hoops. Here is where you play the dilettante, and where it pays to do so. You are, in effect, dropping stones down a well. Every time you hear an echo from your subconscious, you know yourself a little better. A small echo may start an idea. A big echo may result in a story.

What about short stories, novels? Of course. Read those authors who write the way you hope to write, those who think the way you would like to think. But also read those who do not think as you think or write as you want to write, and so be stimulated in directions you might not take for many years. Here again, don't let the snobbery of others prevent you from reading Kipling, say, while no one else is reading him.

Ours is a culture and a time immensely rich in trash as it is in treasures. Sometimes it is a little hard to tell the trash from the treasure, so we hold back, afraid to declare ourselves. But since we are out to give ourselves texture, to collect truths on many levels, and in many ways, to test ourselves against life, and the truths of others, offered us in comic strips, TV shows, books, magazines, newspapers, plays, and films, we should not fear to be seen in strange companies. So what is the pattern that holds all this together? One thing remains always the same: the fever, the ardor, the delight.

I remember wandering, stunned, off a stage in my home town, holding a live rabbit given to me by Blackstone the Magician in the greatest performance ever! I remember wandering, stunned, in the papier-mâché streets of the Century of Progress Exhibition in Chicago in 1933; in the halls of the Venetian doges in Italy in 1954. The quality of each event was immensely different, but my ability to drink it in the same. The constant remains: the search, the finding, the admiration, the love, the honest response to materials at hand, no matter how shabby they one day seem, when looked back on. I sent away for a statue of an African gorilla made of the cheapest ceramics when I was ten, said statue a reward for enclosing the wrapper from a package of Fould's Macaroni. The gorilla, arriving by mail, got a reception as large as that given the Boy David at his first unveiling.

The feeding of the muse then seems to me to be the continual running after loves, the checking of these loves against one's present and future needs, the moving on from simple textures to more complex ones, from naïve ones to more informed ones, from nonintellectual to intellectual ones. Nothing is ever lost. If you have moved over vast territories and dared to love silly things, you will have learned even from the most primitive items collected and put aside in your life. From an ever-roaming curiosity in all the arts, from bad radio to good theater, from nursery rhyme to symphony, from jungle compound to Kafka's *Castle,* there is basic excellence to be winnowed out, truths found, kept, savored, and used on some later day. To be a child of one's time is to do all these things.

Do not, for money, turn away from all the stuff you have collected in a lifetime.

Do not, for the vanity of intellectual publications, turn away from what you are — the material within you which makes you individual, and therefore indispensable to others.

To feed your muse, then, you should always have been hungry about life since you were a child. It means you must still take long walks at night around your city or town, or walks in the country by day. And long walks, at any time, through bookstores and libraries.

And while feeding, how to *keep* your muse is our final problem. By living well, by observing as you live, by reading well and observing as you read, you have fed your most original self. By training yourself in writing, by repetitious exercise, imitation, good example, you have made a clean, well-lighted place to keep the muse. You have given her, him, it, or whatever, room to turn around in. And through training, you have relaxed yourself enough not to stare discourteously when inspiration comes into the room.

You have learned to go immediately to the typewriter and preserve the inspiration for all time by putting it on paper. Look at yourself then. Consider everything you have fed yourself over the years. Was it a banquet or a starvation diet? Who are your friends? Do they believe in you? Or do they stunt your growth with ridicule and disbelief? If the latter, you haven't friends. Go find some.

And finally, have you trained well enough so you can say what you want to say without getting hamstrung? Have you written enough so that you are relaxed and can allow the truth to get out without being ruined by self-conscious posturing or changed by a desire to become rich?

To feed well is to grow. To work well and constantly is to keep what you have learned and know in prime condition. Experience. Labor. These are the twin sides of the coin which when spun is neither experience nor labor, but the moment of revelation. The coin, by optical illusion, becomes a round, bright, whirling globe of life. It is the moment when the porch swing creaks gentle and a voice speaks. All hold their breath. The voice rises and falls. The subconscious stirs and rubs its eyes. The muse ventures in the ferns below the porch, where the summer boys, strewn on the lawn, listen. The words become poetry that no one minds, because no one has thought to call it that. Time is there. Love is there. Story is there. A well-fed man keeps and calmly gives forth his infinitesimal portion of eternity.

It sounds big in the summer night. And it is, as it always was down the ages, when there was a man with something to tell, and ones, quiet and wise, to listen.

Excerpted from Ray Bradbury, *Zen in the Art of Writing* (Santa Barbara, CA: Joshua Odell Editions, 1996), pp. 31–46.

The Creative Process
James Baldwin

Perhaps the primary distinction of the artist is that he must actively cultivate that state which most men, necessarily, must avoid; the state of being alone. That all men are, when the chips are down, alone, is a banality—a banality because it is very frequently stated, but very rarely, on the evidence, believed.

Most of us are not compelled to linger with the knowledge of our aloneness, for it is a knowledge that can paralyze all action in this world. There are, forever, swamps to be drained, cities to be created, mines to be exploited, children to be fed. None of these things can be done alone. But the conquest of the physical world is not man's only duty. He is also enjoined to conquer the great wilderness of himself. The precise role of the artist, then, is to illuminate that darkness, blaze roads through that vast forest, so that we will not, in all our doing, lose sight of its purpose, which is, after all, to make the world a more human dwelling place.

The state of being alone is not meant to bring to mind merely a rustic musing beside some silver lake. The aloneness of which I speak is much more like the aloneness of birth or death. It is like the fearless alone that one sees in the eyes of someone who is suffering, whom we cannot help. Or it is like the aloneness of love, the force and mystery that so many have extolled and so many have cursed, but which no one has ever understood or ever really been able to control.

I put the matter this way, not out of any desire to create pity for the artist—God forbid!—but to suggest how nearly, after all, is his state the state of everyone, and in an attempt to make vivid his endeavor. The state of birth, suffering, love, and death are extreme states—extreme, universal, and inescapable. We all know this, but we would rather not know it. The artist is present to correct the delusions to which we fall prey in our attempts to avoid this knowledge.

It is for this reason that all societies have battled with the incorrigible disturber of the peace—the artist. I doubt that future societies will get on with him any better. The entire purpose of society is to create a bulwark against the inner and the outer chaos, in order to make life bearable and to keep the human race alive. And it is absolutely inevitable that when a tradition has been evolved, whatever the tradition is, the people, in general, will suppose it to have existed from before the beginning of time and will be most unwilling and indeed unable to conceive of any changes in it. They do not know how they will live without those traditions that have given them their identity. Their reaction, when it is suggested that they can or that they must, is panic. And we see this panic, I think, everywhere in the world today, from the streets of New Orleans to the grisly battleground of Algeria. And a higher level of consciousness among the people is the only hope we have, now or in the future, of minimizing human damage.

THE ARTIST IS DISTINGUISHED FROM all other responsible actors in society—the politicians, legislators, educators, and scientists—by the fact that he is his own test tube, his own laboratory, working according to very rigorous rules, however unstated these may be, and cannot allow any consideration to supersede his responsibility to reveal all that he can possibly discover concerning the mystery of the human being. Society must accept some things as real; but he must always know that visible reality hides a deeper one, and that all our action and achievement rest on things unseen. A society must assume that it is stable, but the artist must know, and he must let us know, that there is nothing stable under heaven. One cannot possibly build a school, teach a child, or drive a car without taking some things for granted. The artist cannot and must not take anything for granted, but must drive to the heart of every answer and expose the question the answer hides.

I am really trying to make clear the nature of the artist's responsibility to his society. The peculiar nature of this responsibility is that he must never cease warring with it, for its sake and for his own. For the truth, in spite of appearances and all our hopes, is that everything is always changing and the measure of our maturity as nations and as men is how well prepared we are to meet these changes, and further, to use them for our health.

Now, anyone who has ever been compelled to think about it — anyone, for example, who has ever been in love — knows that the one face that one can never see is one's own face. One's lover — or one's brother, or one's enemy — sees the face you wear, and this face can elicit the most extraordinary reactions. We do the things we do and feel what we feel essentially because we must — we are responsible for our actions, but we rarely understand them. It goes without saying, I believe, that if we understood ourselves better, we would damage ourselves less. But the barrier between oneself and one's knowledge of oneself is high indeed. There are so many things one would rather not know! We become social creatures because we cannot live any other way. But in order to become social, there are a great many other things that we must not become, and we are frightened, all of us, of these forces within us that perpetually menace our precarious security. Yet the forces are there: we cannot will them away. All we can do is learn to live with them. And we cannot learn this unless we are willing to tell the truth about ourselves, and the truth about us is always at variance with what we wish to be. The human effort is to bring these two realities into a relationship resembling reconciliation. The human beings whom we respect the most, after all — and sometimes fear the most — are those who are most deeply involved in this delicate and strenuous effort, for they have the unshakable authority that comes only from having looked on and endured and survived the worst. That nation is healthiest which has the least necessity to distrust or ostracize these people — whom, as I say, we honor, once they are gone, because somewhere in our hearts we know that we cannot live without them.

THE DANGERS OF BEING AN American artist are not greater than those of being an artist anywhere else in the world, but they are very particular. These dangers are produced by our history. They rest on the fact that in order to conquer this continent, the particular aloneness of which I speak — the aloneness in which one discovers that life is tragic, and therefore unutterably beautiful — could not be permitted. And that this prohibition is typical of all emergent nations will be proved, I have no doubt, in many ways during the next fifty years. This continent now is conquered, but our habits and our fears remain. And, in the same way that to become a social human being one modifies and suppresses and, ultimately, without great courage, lies to oneself about all one's interior, uncharted chaos, so have we, as a nation, modified or suppressed and lied about all the darker forces in our history. We know, in the case of the person, that whoever cannot tell himself the truth about his past is trapped in it, is immobilized in the prison of his undiscovered self. This is also true of nations. We know how a person, in such a paralysis, is unable to assess either his weaknesses or his strengths, and how frequently indeed he mistakes the one for the other. And this, I think, we do. We are the strongest nation in the Western world, but this is not for the reasons that we think. It is because we have an opportunity that no other nation has in moving beyond the Old World concepts of race and class and caste, to create, finally, what we must have had in mind when we first began speaking of the New World. But the price of this is a long look backward to when we came and an unflinching assessment of the record. For an artist, the record of that journey is most clearly revealed in the personalities of the people the journey produced. Societies never know it, but the war of an artist with his society is a lover's war, and he does, at his best, what lovers do, which is to reveal the beloved to himself and, with that revelation, to make freedom real.

James Baldwin, "The Creative Process," in *Creative America* (New York: Ridge Press, 1962), pp. 17–21.

The Psychomagic of Cinema
Alejandro Jodorowsky

I don't know myself. The human being is infinite. We never really know each other completely. We find out who we are, gradually, while creating things. So I can't define myself as a whole. If I could, it would mean I'm dying. But I plan to live to be one hundred and twenty years old. I've loved my entire life and have always done what I wanted to do. And I have worked with people I loved. I've always been true to myself and never listened to what others wanted me to be.

My backbone is poetry, and poetry is nothing more than the search for beauty. We seek out truth with language as our guide, but we can't find truth this way. Words are not the thing. And though philosophy is a search for truth, it is not the truth. We attempt the search through language. But beauty is what I'm after. So let's search for beauty!

In Greek mythology, the Three Graces always go together and can't be separated. They are truth, beauty, and goodness. If a truth contains neither beauty nor goodness then it's not the truth. There are no evil truths. If it is as they say, that life is an illusion, then it's the most beautiful of all illusions. The Three Graces belong together, and this is what I look for in my films—truth, sublime beauty, and goodness.

CINEMA IS THE MOST COMPLETE of all the arts. But it's a business and was born to make money. It's expensive to make a film. First you need to find money to finance it. This is very difficult, almost impossible, especially if you'd rather make art than business. I've always been a kind of extraterrestrial, a stranger.

When I see so many films presented at festivals, I have an attack of modesty, because there are so many people expressing themselves, and it's difficult for them to do so freely as filmmakers. There are always producers around, and that's the first thing you have to fight against. Then there are the movie stars — the second thing you have to fight against. There will always be economic problems and all the other difficulties associated with making films.

I made my last film, *Endless Poetry* (and the previous one, *The Dance of Reality*),[1] in a country that for me had become foreign, because I hadn't been to Chile and the places where I once lived in sixty years. And I had only two months to prepare the film. What does it mean to prepare a film? You have to choose the performers, for instance, who are not always famous actors but regular people. You have

---

1 *The Dance of Reality* (2013) is Jodorowsky's fantasy film based on his 2001 book *The Dance of Reality: A Psychomagical Autobiography* (*La danza de la realidad: Psicomagia y psicochamanismo*). The sequel, *Endless Poetry* (*Poesía sin fin*, 2016), continues the autobiographical story of an aspiring poet's quest for beauty and personal truth.

two months to build sets and create hundreds of costumes. Two months to find every little object that appears in the film (which I prefer to find myself). It's a crazy job. And then you have thirty-five days to shoot a two-hour film which will compete against major productions. You can't miss a shot; if you get it wrong you often can't repeat it since there's no money allocated for mistakes. We film everything in thirty-five days and experience all the miracles that occur during filming. It's really difficult. But what a pleasure. It's a continuous orgasm.

THERE ARE TERRIBLE MIRACLES THAT occur when making films. I can tell you a couple of anecdotes related to *Endless Poetry.* In the film, the grandmother had to be a strong and awful woman. To play the role, I chose a seventy-year-old actress who had once been a movie star and who cost me an entire day, which meant fifty thousand dollars, because she didn't know her part and because she was considered a great actress. She's the only one I was wrong about, but it was a disaster for the film. I called her at midnight and said to her, "Listen, *Señora*, you are what you are but you don't know the role. It's a shame but tomorrow you have to read your lines. We'll make large cue cards like the ones Marlon Brando used." But the next day she didn't appear on the set. "Go find her! … She won't open her door. … Break it down!" And there she was, dead. So another actress played the aunt and I knew she was the right person for the part, so we started filming her right away. A perfectly terrible miracle.

THERE'S A FEELING, TODAY, THAT commercial cinema thinks young people are idiots. They say, "Look at how they play Pokémon, those idiots!" They say that's how they are, that they don't think. So they make films for idiots.

I once gave my script to a big production company in Hollywood. They asked me for fifty copies. "Why so many?" "It's for the fifty idiots we hire to read it, to see if the film will be understood." Of course, they decided not to make the film.

But if you follow the festivals, you learn that young people want to make films and arrive at an art that speaks of human value. They're tired of chases, gunshots, miserable young lovers, superheroes, wars, politics, social problems. They can't take it anymore; they want a profound cinema that explains what life is about, why we're alive, what our purpose is. That's the fundamental question: what is your purpose in life?

When I finished shooting *The Holy Mountain*,[2] I ran away from Mexico because they threatened me with death. I went to New York to edit, and every night I started sweating

---

2 Jodorowsky's surrealist film *The Holy Mountain* (*La montaña sagrada*, 1973) takes the form of a spiritual search for enlightenment, where illusion is in conflict with the truth.

profusely. I was sick! So I went to a Chinese doctor who held free consultations, a man who looked like he was a hundred years old. And he said to me: "What is your purpose in life?" I replied, "Sir, I'm sick. I don't want to talk about philosophy." And he said, "If you have no clear purpose in life, I can't cure you."

YOU THINK SOMEONE'S CRAZY WHEN they do something you don't understand. But when you don't understand something, just study it. Sometimes we think a person's crazy and then we discover that we're the ones who are crazy.

When I read the *Tractatus* by Wittgenstein—the greatest philosopher of the twentieth century—I didn't understand anything. It took me years. Every day I tried again to understand. This has done me a great deal of good. Wittgenstein was no fool; he was a genius. The same thing with the seventy-eight tarot cards: the cards, I was told, contain all the wisdom in the world, but I didn't understand anything. So I began to study them. Instead of spurning them, I studied them for forty years and now I've come to understand them. I never call what is bizarre or what I don't understand crazy, but I'll always ask myself, "Why is this so?" Madness is basically a myth. It's not a disease; it's a different cerebral ability which sometimes becomes neurosis. Maybe we're all neurotic.

HOW DO YOU FREE YOURSELF from prejudices? Through suffering. You suffer a lot by putting yourself in certain situations where you can't decide, in the abstract, what to do to solve the problem. You might wonder, for example, what the Buddha would do in such a situation, what a perfect being would do. We have incredible things within us. We have inner guides who are there to give us advice. There's no better adviser than oneself. That's why we have to learn to love each other. This is the most important thing: love yourself like you love others. I am as I am and others are free to be as they are. You have to recognize the value in other people. If you don't, you won't progress. Realize that we never own anything entirely. Know that we're all connected, that we're all part of a larger community. We're not the American hero who alone changes the world. We're part of a whole. When we understand this, we realize that we're constituted by an artificial ego, created by one's family, society, and by history, but also by an essential, authentic being.

Usually, we follow the ego. We must instead make sure that the ego follows us. You advance with your sense of truth and the ego comes after you. At that point, learning to live with the truth is simple.

I HAD A TWENTY-FOUR-YEAR-OLD SON who died of an overdose. It was terrible. Really terrible. So nobody can tell me that my life has been wonderful. And I emerged from my various marriages in a very bad state. When you're with a person who isn't a good match, it's hell on earth.

And then there are cinematic failures. I made a film called *Tusk* about an elephant. A disaster. They made me sign a contract agreeing to certain things they wanted in the film—for example, a fight between two elephants. And the fight had to be shot from no further than fifteen meters away. How can that be filmed? The producer used the money to buy an airplane and a Porsche. And the result is a horrible film.

I carry all this as a wound in my soul. You can't say that everything's good—although terrible events can be seen in different ways, depending on your interpretation. They can even nourish you. Misery is like a trampoline; the lower you sink the higher you rise.

Excerpted from an audio transcript of Alejandro Jodorowsky speaking at the Locarno Film Festival in Locarno, Switzerland, August 2016. Translated by Peter Valente.

Bottle by Bottle
Robert Irwin

When you look at the work, you think he's painting bottles, little still-life paintings, but they weren't. Morandi[1] came in the back door. It was almost a Zen activity. He painted the same bottles over and over and over, so it wasn't really about bottles anymore. If he was a still-life painter, he wouldn't have painted the same bottles over and over.

They're about painting — the figure–ground relationship, structure and organization. Morandi's were paintings in the purest sense of the word. They were like a mantra, repeated over and over until it was divorced from words and became pure sounds.

---

1   Italian still-life painter and printmaker Giorgio Morandi (1890–1964) was known for his meticulous renderings of simple household objects.—*Ed.*

Excerpted from an interview with Robert Irwin by Leah Ollman, "Giorgio Morandi, Bottle by Bottle," *Los Angeles Times* (November 9, 2008).

On Looking
Edmund de Waal

Tschirnhaus[1] thinks that it is possible to analyze the products of the arts in a philosophical manner—that boats, bridges, and buildings should be considered as arts of invention. These objects can train what he calls the "active imagination" because they exhibit "all the possibilities to the imagination." In fact, I realize, he takes on the world as possibility—as you walk down the street there is nothing in the material world that you encounter that cannot be brought into this space of reflection. And at each point of this reflection, as you pause and look with dedication at this lamp post, that gateway, you recreate the manner of its creation, move through the series of actions that caused it to come into being.

Above all he is interested, he writes, in "how to obtain what should be observed," in the "first mode of formation" of things. Tschirnhaus is describing with a passionate lucidity the value of looking and thinking about how an object as an idea comes into being.

Spinoza holds ideas and decisions only valid if they are *sub specie aeternitatis*, from the perspective of eternity. Newton's prescription is to inquire diligently into the

---

1 Ehrenfried Walther von Tschirnhaus (1651–1708) was a German mathematician, physicist, and philosopher, considered by some to have invented European porcelain.—*Ed.*

properties of things, and Leibniz writes in a tremendous letter to Tschirnhaus that "no one should fear that the contemplation of characters will lead us away from things themselves: on the contrary it leads us into the interior of things." He talks of *rei naturam intimam*, the inner nature of the thing. Interiority has become an idea.

And for Tschirnhaus, philosopher and mathematician and observer of how the world changes, porcelain is an idea to be scrutinized. It is compelling as it is a seemingly intractable white material through which light can pass: it brings together two of the principal concerns of his fellow philosophers, China and light, into one great query.

Excerpted from Edmund de Waal, "The First Mode of Formation" in *The White Road* (London: Chatto & Windus, 2015), pp. 140–141.

Chopin at the Piano
Robert Schumann

And I explained that it was indeed an unforgettable image of Chopin sitting at the piano like a dreaming clairvoyant, and how, listening to him play, one felt oneself becoming the very dream he was creating, and how he had the hopeless habit, after the end of each piece, of running one finger across the keys of the still reverberating piano, as if to release himself from his dream by force.

Excerpted from Robert Schumann, "Bericht von Jeanquirit in Augsburg über den letzten kunsthistorischen Ball beim Redakteur," *Neue Zeitschrift für Musik* [New Journal of Music] 6, no. 40 (May 19, 1837), p. 160. Translated from the German by Janos Tedeschi.

Simplicity
Frédéric Chopin

Simplicity is the final achievement. After one has conquered all the difficulties, after one has played a vast quantity of notes and more notes, it is simplicity that emerges in all its charm as the ultimate crowning reward of art.

Frédéric Chopin quoted in Willard A. Palmer, ed., *Chopin: An Introduction to His Piano Works* (New York: Alfred Publishing Co., 1971), p. 4.

The Printed Word in Peril
Will Self

In February, at an event at the 92nd Street Y's Unterberg Poetry Center in New York, while sharing the stage with my fellow British writer Martin Amis and discussing the impact of screen-based reading and bidirectional digital media[1] on the Republic of Letters, I threw this query out to an audience that I estimate was about three hundred strong: "Have any of you been reading anything by Norman Mailer in the past year?" After a while, one hand went up, then another tentatively semi-elevated. Frankly I was surprised it was that many. Of course, there are good reasons why Mailer in particular should suffer posthumous obscurity with such alacrity: his brand of male essentialist braggadocio is arguably extraneous in the age of Weinstein and fourth-wave feminism. Moreover, Mailer's brilliance, such as it was, seemed, even at the time he wrote, to be sparks struck by a steely intellect against the tortuous rocks of a particular age, even though he labored tirelessly to the very end, principally as the booster of his own reputation.

It's also true that, as J. G. Ballard sagely remarked, for a writer, death is always a career move, and for most of us the move is a demotion, as simultaneously we're lowered

---

1 By *bidirectional digital media*, I mean the suite of technologies that comprises the wireless-connected computer, handheld or otherwise, the World Wide Web, and the Internet.

into the grave and our works into the dustbin. But having noted all of the above, it remains the case that Mailer's death coincided with another far greater extinction: that of the literary milieu in which he'd come to prominence and been sustained for decades. It's a milieu that I hesitate to identify entirely with what's understood by the ringing phrase "the Republic of Letters," even though the overlap between the two was once great indeed; and I cannot be alone in wondering what will remain of the latter once the former, which not long ago seemed so very solid, has melted into air.

What I do feel isolated in — if not entirely alone in — is my determination, as a novelist, essayist, and journalist, not to rage against the dying of literature's light, although it's surprising how little of this there is, but merely to examine the great technological discontinuity of our era, as we pivot from the wave to the particle, the fractal to the fungible, and the mechanical to the computable. I first began consciously responding, as a literary practitioner, to the manifold impacts of bidirectional digital media in the early 2000s — although, being the age I am, I have been feeling its effects throughout my working life — and I first started to write and speak publicly about it around a decade ago. Initially I had the impression I was being heard out, if reluctantly, but as the years have passed, my attempts to limn the shape of this epochal transformation have been met increasingly with outrage, and even abuse, in particular from my fellow writers.

As for my attempts to express the impact of the screen on the page, on the actual pages of literary novels, I now understand that these were altogether irrelevant to the requirement of the age that everything be easier, faster, and slicker in order to compel the attention of screen viewers. It strikes me that we're now suffering collectively from a "tyranny of the virtual," since we find ourselves unable to look away from the screens that mediate not just print but, increasingly, reality itself.

As I survey the great *Götterdämmerung* of the Gutenberg half-millennium, what comes to mind is the hopeful finale to Ray Bradbury's *Fahrenheit 451.* When Guy Montag, the onetime "fireman" or burner of books by appointment to a dystopian totalitarian state, falls in among the dissident hobo underclass, he finds them to be the saviors of those books, each person having memorized some or all of a lost and incalculably precious volume—one person *Gulliver's Travels*; another the Book of Ecclesiastes.

In March, I gave an interview to the *Guardian* in which I repeated my usual—and unwelcome—assertion that the literary novel had quit center stage of our culture and was in the process, via university creative-writing programs, of becoming a conservatory form, like the easel painting or the symphony. Furthermore, I fingered bidirectional digital media as responsible for this transformation, the literary novel being simply the canary forced to flee this particular mine shaft first. The response was a Twitter storm of predictable vehemence and more than seven hundred comments on the *Guardian*'s website, which, reading over preparatory to writing this article, I found to display all the characteristics of the modern online debate: willful misunderstanding and misinterpretation of my original statements, together with criticism that is either *ad hominem* or else transparently animated by a superimposed ideological cleavage.

Some critics comment that the literary novel has always been a marginal cultural form; others, that its torchbearers are now from outside the mainstream Western tradition, either by reason of ethnicity, heritage, sex, or sexual orientation. Both these and others aver that the novel form is alive and kicking, that paperback sales have actually risen in the past few years, and that readers are rediscovering the great virtues of the printed word as a media technology.

All of these viewpoints I'm more than willing to entertain. What I'm less prepared to consider are arguments that begin by quoting sales figures that show the sales of printed books increasing and those of e-books in decline. The printed books being sold are not the sort of difficult reading that spearheads knowledge transfer but picture books, kidult novels like the Harry Potter series, and, in the case of my own UK publisher at least, a great tranche of spin-off books by so-called vloggers (a development Marshall McLuhan anticipated when he noted that new media always cannibalize the forms of the past). As for the decline in e-books, this is because the screen is indeed not a good vehicle for the delivery of long-form prose; and anyway the printed literary novel (or otherwise challenging text) is competing not with its digital counterparts but with computer-generated games, videos, social media, and all the other entertainments the screen affords. Moreover, I'd wager that the upsurge in printed-book sales, such as it is, is due to greater exports and the continuation of, in the West at least, a strange demographic reversal, since for the first time in history we have societies where the old significantly outnumber the young.

Be all this as it may, in December of last year an authoritative report was delivered on behalf of Arts Council England. Undertaken by the digital publisher Canelo, it compiled and analyzed sales data from Nielsen BookScan demonstrating that between 2007 and 2011 hardcover fiction sales in England slumped by ten million pounds (approximately thirteen million US dollars), while paperback fiction suffered still more, with year-on-year declines almost consistently since 2008. In one year alone, 2011–2012, paperback fiction sales fell by twenty-six percent.

There is, of course, a great deal of empirical research concerning the impact of screen media on the mind/brain, but for this essay I concentrated on a couple of academic papers coauthored by a Norwegian education researcher, Professor Anne Mangen of the Norwegian Reading Centre, based at the University of Stavanger. One paper is titled "Lost in an iPad: Narrative Engagement on Paper and Tablet"; the other, "Reading Linear Texts on Paper Versus Computer Screen: Effects on Reading Comprehension." The papers covered two studies, one conducted with Canadian university students in 2014, the other in 2013 with Norwegian high-school students, in which screen reading and paper reading were compared.

Mangen's papers suggest that as our capacity for narrative engagement is compromised by new technology, we experience less "transportation" (the term for being "lost" in a piece of writing), and as a further consequence become less capable of experiencing empathy. Why? Because evidence from real-time brain scans tells us that when we become deeply engaged with reading about Anna Karenina's adultery, at a neural level it looks pretty much as if we were committing that adultery ourselves, such is the congruence in the areas of the brain activated. Of course, book lovers have claimed since long before the invention of brain scanning that identifying with characters in stories makes us better able to appreciate the feelings of real live humans, though this certainly seems to be a case of correlation being substituted for causation. People of sensibility have always been readers, which is by no means to say reading made them so—and who's to say my empathy centers don't light up when Anna throws herself to her death because I take a malevolent satisfaction in her ruin?

Nicholas Carr's *The Shallows* reaches a baleful crescendo with this denunciation: the automation of our own mental processes will result in "a slow erosion of our humanness and our humanity" as our intelligence "flattens into artificial intelligence." Which seems to me a warning that the so-called singularity envisaged by techno-utopians such as Ray Kurzweil, a director of engineering at Google, may come about involuntarily, simply as a function of our using our smartphones too much. Because the neuroscientific evidence is now compelling and confirmed by hundreds, if not thousands, of studies: our ever-increasing engagement with bidirectional digital media is substantially reconfiguring our mind/brains, while the new environments it creates—referred to now as code/space, since these are locations that are themselves mediated by software—may well be the crucible for epigenetic changes that are heritable. Behold! The age of *Homo virtualis* is quite likely upon us, and while this may be offensive to those of us who believe humans to have been made in God's image, it's been received as a cause for rejoicing for those who believe God to be some sort of cosmic computer.

But what might it be like to limit or otherwise modulate our interaction with bidirectional digital media so as to retain some of the cognitive virtues of paper-based knowledge technology? Can we envisage computer–human interactions that are more multisensory so as to preserve our awareness and our memory? For whatever publishers may say now about the survival of print (and with it their expense accounts), the truth is that the economies of scale, production, and distribution render the spread of digital text ineluctable, even if long-form narrative prose were to continue as one of humanity's dominant modes of knowledge transfer. But of course it won't. It was one of Marshall McLuhan's most celebrated insights that the mode of knowledge transfer is more significant than the knowledge itself: "The medium is the message."

For decades now, theorists from a variety of disciplines have been struggling to ascertain the message of bidirectional digital media considered as a medium, a task hampered by its multifarious character: Is it a television, a radio, an electronic newspaper, a videophone, or none of the above? McLuhan distinguished confusingly between "hot" and "cold" media—ones that complement human perception and ones that provoke human sensual imagination—but bidirectional digital media holds out the prospect of content that's terminally lukewarm: a refashioning of perception that will render imagination effectively obsolete. In place of the collective, intergenerational experience of reading *Moby Dick,* centuries-long virtualities will be compressed to the bandwidth of real time and fed to us via headsets and all-body feely suits, "us" being the operative word. With a small volume in your pocket, you may well wander lonely as a cloud, stop, get it out, and read about another notionally autonomous wanderer. But the Prelude Experience, a Wordsworthian virtual-reality program I invented just this second, requires your own wearable tech, the armies of coders — human or machine — necessary to write it, and the legions of computers, interconnected by a convolvulus of fiber-optic cabling, needed to make it seem to happen.

What the critics of bidirectional digital media fear most is the loss of their own autonomous Gutenberg minds, minds that, like the books they're in symbiosis with, can be shut up and put away in a pocket, minds the operations of which can be hidden from Orwellian surveillance. But the message of bidirectional digital media is that the autonomous human mind was itself a contingent feature of a particular technological era.

BY CONTRAST WITH THE ANONYMOUS and tacit intimacy to be found between hard covers, social media is all about stridently identified selves — and not simply to one another but to all. In the global village of social media it's precisely those contingent factors of our identities — our sex, our race, our class, our nationality — that loom largest; no wonder it's been the medium that has both formed and been formed by the new politics of identity.

And are we not witnessing a flowering of talent and a clamor of new voices? Is not women's writing and writing by those coming from the margins receiving the kind of attention it deserved for years but was denied by this heteronormative, patriarchal, paper-white hegemony? One of the strongest and most credible counters to the argument that in transitioning from page to screen we lost the art forms that arose in and were dependent on that medium is that this is simply the nostalgia of a group who for too long occupied the apex of a pyramid, the base of which ground others into the dust. Younger and more diverse writers are now streaming into the public forums — whether virtual or actual — and populating them with their stories, their realities; and all this talk of death by iPad is simply the sound of old men (and a few women) shaking their fists at the cloud.

In this historical moment, it perhaps seems that the medium is irrelevant; the prevalence of creative-writing programs and the self-published online text taken together seem to me to represent a strange new formula arrived at by the elision of two aphoristic observations: this permanent Now is indeed the future in which everyone is famous for fifteen minutes — and famous for the novel that everyone was also assured they had in them. How can the expansion of the numbers writing novels — or at least attempting to write them — not be a good thing? Maybe it is, but it's not writing as we knew it; it's not the carving out of new conceptual and imaginative space, it's not the boldly solo going but rather a sort of recursive quilting, in which the community of writers enacts solidarity through the reading of one another's texts.

For in a cultural arena such as this, the avant-garde ends mathematically, as the number of writers moves from being an arithmetic to a geometric coefficient of the number of readers. We know intuitively that we live in a world where you can say whatever you want—because no one's listening. A *skeuomorph* is the term for a once functional object that has, because of technological change, been repurposed to be purely decorative. A good example of this is the crude pictogram of an old-fashioned telephone that constitutes the "phone" icon on the screen of your handheld computer (also known, confusingly, as a smartphone).

Skeuomorphs tend, for obvious reasons, to proliferate precisely at the point where one technology gives ground to another. I put it to you that the contemporary novel is now a skeuomorphic form, and that its proliferation is indeed due to this being the moment of its transformation from the purposive to the decorative. Who is writing these novels, and what for, is beside the point. Moreover, the determination to effect cultural change—by the imposition of diversity quotas—is itself an indication of printed paper's looming redundancy. Unlike the British novelist Howard Jacobson, who recently took it upon himself to blame the reader for the decline in sales of literary fiction, rather than the obsolescence of its means of reproduction, I feel no inclination to blame anyone at all: this is beyond good and evil.

At the end of Bradbury's *Fahrenheit 451,* the exiled hoboes return to the cities, which have been destroyed by the nuclear conflicts of the illiterate, bringing with them their head-borne texts, ready to restart civilization. And it's this that seems to me the most prescient part of Bradbury's menacing vision. For I see no future for the words printed on paper, or the art forms they enacted, if our civilization continues on this digital trajectory: there's no way back to the future—especially not through the portal of a printed text.

The World Out There
Ray Bradbury

The men lay gasping like fish laid out on the grass. They held to the earth as children hold to familiar things, no matter how cold or dead, no matter what has happened or will happen, their fingers were clawed into the dirt, and they were all shouting to keep their eardrums from bursting, to keep their sanity from bursting, mouths open, Montag shouting with them, a protest against the wind that ripped their faces and tore at their lips, making their noses bleed.

Montag watched the great dust settle and the great silence move down upon their world. And lying there it seemed that he saw every single grain of dust and every blade of grass and that he heard every cry and shout and whisper going up in the world now. Silence fell down in the sifting dust, and all the leisure they might need to look around, to gather the reality of this day into their senses.

Montag looked at the river. We'll go on the river. He looked at the old railroad tracks. Or we'll go that way. Or we'll walk on the highways now, and we'll have time to put things into ourselves. And some day, after it sets in us a long time, it'll come out of our hands and our mouths. And a lot of it will be wrong, but just enough of it will be right. We'll just start walking today and see the world and the way the world walks around and talks, the way it really looks. I want to see everything now. And while none of it will be me when it goes in, after a while it'll all gather together inside and it'll be me. Look at the world out there, my God, my God, look at it out there, outside me, out there beyond my face and the only way to really touch it is to put it where it's finally me, where it's in the blood, where it pumps around a thousand times ten thousand a day. I get hold of it so it'll never run off. I'll hold on to the world tight some day. I've got one finger on it now; that's a beginning.

Ray Bradbury, *Fahrenheit 451* (New York: Simon & Schuster, 1951), p. 154–155.

Dancing with the Dead
Red Pine

Every time I translate a book of poems, I learn a new way of dancing. The people with whom I dance, though, are the dead—not the recently departed, but people who have been dead a long time. A thousand years or so seems about right. And the music has to be Chinese. It's the only music I've learned to dance to.

I'm not sure what led me to this conclusion, that translation is like dancing. Buddhist meditation. Language theory. Cognitive psychology. Drugs. Sex. Rock and roll. My ruminations on the subject go back more than twenty-five years to when I was first living in Taiwan. One day I was browsing through the pirated editions at Caves Bookstore in Taipei, and I picked up a copy of Allen Ginsberg's *Howl*. It was like trying to make sense of hieroglyphics. I put it back down and looked for something else. Then a friend loaned me a video of Ginsberg reading the poem. What a difference. In Ginsberg's voice, I heard the energy and rhythm, the sound and silence, the vision, the poetry. It was the same with Gary Snyder—his poems only resonated with me once I heard him read them aloud. The words on a page, I concluded, are not the poem. They are the recipe, not the meal; steps drawn on a dance floor, not the dance.

For the past hundred thousand years or so, we human beings have developed language as our primary means of communication—first spoken language and more recently written language. We have used language to convey information to each other, to communicate. But there is a set of questions just below the surface. How well does language do what we think it does? And what exactly does it do? We prefer not to address such questions because language is so mercurial. We can never quite pin it down. It is forever in flux, because we, its speakers and writers and translators, are forever in flux. We might use or read or hear the same word twice, but we can't step into precisely the same thought a second time. We speak of language as if it were a fixed phenomenon, and we teach it and learn it as if it were carved in stone. But it is more like water, because we are more like water. Language is at the surface of the much deeper flow of our riverine minds. Thus, if we approach translation by focusing on language alone, we mistake the ripples for the river, the tracks for the journey.

But this isn't all. A number of linguists and anthropologists are of the opinion that language was developed by early humans not simply for the purpose of communication but also for deception. All beings communicate, but only humans deceive each other. And for such deception, we rely primarily on language. It isn't easy for us to hide our feelings and intentions in facial or bodily expressions, but language offers endless opportunities for altering and manipulating the truth. The primary concern of a translator is not the efficiency of language, therefore, but its truthfulness. That is, does it actually do what we think it does, and does it do this in any context other than fiction?

We live in worlds of linguistic fabrication. Pine trees do not grow with the word "pine" hanging from their branches. Nor does a pine tree "welcome" anyone to its shade. It is we who decide what words to use, and, like Alice, what they mean. And what they mean does not necessarily have anything to do with reality. They are sleights of the mind as well as the hand and the lips. And if we mistake words for reality, they are no longer simply sleights but lies. Yet, if we can see them for what they are, if we can see beyond their deception, they are like so many crows on the wing, disappearing with the setting sun into the trees beyond our home. This is what poetry does. It brings us closer to the truth. Not all the way to the truth, for language wilts in such light, but close enough to feel the heat.

According to the Great Preface of the *Book of Odes*, the Chinese character for poetry means "words from the heart." This would seem to be a characteristic of poetry in other cultures as well — that it comes from the heart, unlike prose, which comes from the head. While prose retains the deceptive quality of language, poetry is our ancient and ongoing attempt to transcend language, to overcome its deceptive nature by exploring and exposing the deeper levels of our consciousness and our emotions. Though poetry is still mediated by language, it involves a minimal use of words, and it also weakens the dominance of language through such elements as sound and silence, rhythm and harmony, elements more common to music than logic. In poetry, we come as close as we are likely to get to the meaning and to the heart of another person.

This, too, isn't all. Poetry is not simply "words from the heart." A poet doesn't make a poem so much as discover one, maybe in a garden or a ghetto, maybe in a garbage dump or a government corridor, or in a galaxy of stars. In poetry, we go beyond ourselves to the heart of the universe, where we might be moved by something as small as a grain of sand or as great as the Ganges.

So what does all this mean for the translator? For me it means that I cannot simply limit myself to the words I find on the page. I have to go deeper, to dive into the river. If language is our greatest collective lie, poetry is our attempt to undo that deception. When I translate a poem, I think of the Chinese on the page not as the poem but as evidence that the poem exists. Poetry shows itself in words, and words are how we know it. But words are only the surface. Even after poets give their discoveries expression in language, they continue to discover a poem's deeper nuances, and they make changes: maybe a few words, maybe a few lines, maybe much more. The poem, as I see it, is a never-ending process of discovery. And it isn't just language. It's the unspoken vision that impels a poet and to which the poet tries to give expression, even if that expression can only ever be incomplete, just a few fragments from a kaleidoscopic insight, a few steps on the dance floor impelled by music even the poet hears only imperfectly.

Then a translator comes along and things change. It is only then that the poet no longer dances alone but with a partner. And together they manifest deeper insight into the poem, into the music that motivates the dance. I have come to realize that translation is not just another literary art, it is the *ultimate* literary art, the ultimate challenge in both understanding and performance. For me, this means a tango with Li Bai, a waltz with Wei Yingwu, a dance with the dead.

The Tree Rustled
E. M. Forster

The present flowed by them like a stream. The tree rustled. It had made music before they were born, and would continue after their deaths, but its song was of the moment. The moment had passed. The tree rustled again. Their senses were sharpened, and they seemed to apprehend life. Life passed. The tree rustled again.

E. M. Forster, *Howards End* (New York: Alfred A. Knopf, 1921), p. 361.

Everyday Profundity
John Landau

What I desire is a return to the profundity of experience. I want a society where everyday activity, however mundane, is centered around how incredibly profound everything is. I want that profundity to become so immense that any mediations between us and it become totally unnecessary: we are in the marvel.

Why are we here? *To experience profoundly.* Our task, therefore, is to rearrange society and the economy such that profundity is *immanent* in everyday life. Spirituality has come to represent specialization and detachment of profundity from everyday life into a disembodied, disconnected, symbolic realm that becomes compensatory for an everyday life whose immanence is banality. It is obvious that we don't regularly experience wonder, and this is a social–material problem, because the structure of everyday life discourages this.

We wish to make calculation and obligation islands in a sea of wonder and awe. We wish to make aloneness a positive experience within the context of profound, embodied togetherness.

We are discussing a life where one gives joy to others through the mere act of being, where exchange of gifts is a way of life, where one's routine has inherent meaning, not because it makes reference to some symbolic system, but because it opens one out onto *kairos*,[1] the profound moment, the experience of ambience, awe.

In order to do this, we must develop a *pace* that is conducive to this, a set of understandings whereby the experience of profundity is a value and for which rests, pauses, and meditations are part of routine, so that social reality is based upon sharing of profound experience as primary exchange rather than the exchange of money or etiquette.

Silence was a great future of earlier times. People gestured towards the world. Experiences of awe, wonder were everyday affairs. Because people lived outside, they had a much greater oxygen content. They lived in a perpetual oxygen bath, which produces highs, heightens the sense of taste and smell, and is very relaxing. Anyone who has camped out in the open air knows this experience.

The energetic connection with the surroundings was immense; an incredible exchange on all levels was constantly taking place. What Zen practitioners strive for over a lifetime, our ancestors had by birthright.

In the silence, all of the chitchat and all of the worries and all of the monuments fade. In the is-ness, what need to leave one's mark? What need to become immortal through art or culture? Disappearance is erasing the record: off track,

---

1 From Greek καιρός meaning "right or proper time. The propitious moment for the performance of an action or the coming into being of a new state." *Oxford English Dictionary*, 2nd ed. (1989), s.v. "kairos."—*Ed.*

no trails, no history. One is in the disappearance already. All one needs is to lose track, to stop recording, to turn off the tape machine, to disappear. It's all right; it's OK to disappear. Do so now. The grass in front of you is all that ever was or will be. It has no memory, no future. Just silence.

Contemplate the Fire
Hermann Hesse

Contemplate the fire, contemplate the clouds, and when omens appear and voices begin to sound in your soul, abandon yourself to them without wondering beforehand whether it seems convenient or good to do so. If you hesitate, you will spoil your own being, you will become little more than the bourgeois façade which encloses you, and you will become a fossil.

Hermann Hesse, *Demian: The Story of Emil Sinclair's Youth*, quoted in Miguel Serrano, *C.G. Jung and Hermann Hesse: A Record of Two Friendships,* trans. Frank MacShane (London: Routledge, 1966), p.6.

Seeing Beyond the Periphery
Trebbe Johnson

When I was in my mid twenties, a garden at twilight told me a secret. It taught me how to see the wondrous amidst its camouflage, and it was a lesson that's guided me ever since.

I had fallen in love with the old stone cottage the minute I first saw it. It was in a tiny English village of about one hundred and fifty people and it faced the Berkshire Downs, those hills that ripple out endlessly under the sky. Not far away was the famous Uffington White Horse, a stylized horse carved into the chalk on a hillside a thousand years before. Before I even went inside the cottage, I loved it for the garden—a tangled, overgrown, wild patch that ran all the way from the road up to the gabled door. Lilies, roses, bachelor buttons were in bloom. It made me think of *The Secret Garden,* a book I had loved as a child. I had always hoped to stumble upon my own secret garden, and this seemed to be it.

I moved in on midsummer's day and planned to spend as long as I had in the cottage writing. So that evening I began creating a desk for myself out of an old wooden door and two sturdy crates. I was upstairs in front of the open casement windows and it was late, maybe nine o'clock. The June nights came on slowly that far north, but the downs were finally settling into shadow.

Then, at the periphery of my attention, something began to glow. I looked up from my desk to see what it was. A patch of lilies, which had been white as starlight in the day, now flared silver in the bluing twilight. All the plants in the garden had faded to dark except those lilies, which looked at that moment as if they were radiating back into the oncoming night some of the sun they had absorbed by day. And then, as I marveled at this botanical perseverance, the lilies were extinguished. The color simply faded and all the garden was plunged into night.

I was stunned. I knew I had witnessed something extra-ordinary. It was as if I had peered through a crack in a door and beheld an exalted place—a queen's palace or a lama's cave. And in that instant I understood that if I were to pay attention to the spaces between and just behind the things I thought I needed to look at, there was no limit to what I might witness.

The Collector
Matthew Hollis

Seek rarity as old men might seek time.
By which you meant such glimpses in the grasses:

a fledgling bittern, a Norfolk Hawker,
an earthstar last seen in the war;

and now a scarce fen orchid,
found on just three sites you will not name.

I've seen it, in the reed beds of the alder carr,
staked to keep it out from under foot.

You'd barely note its modesty:
its simple, yellow-greening flowers,

its humble leaves, unscented airs,
so well within the frame of ordinary.

But scarcity can lend a mind to madness,
to strain to keep in harness what runs out.

In these numb unnumbered mornings,
our tea-bags clouding in the cup,

what's common is suddenly so precious:
this sunburst through a pane of glass;

an arrow of geese
pointed somewhere south;

the toddler in the street below
who looks so far to see just up ahead,

his eyeline tilted skyward,
reaching out an ungloved hand for rain.

Where Did the Time Go?
Nina Simone

We are recording tonight. And because we are recording, we're trying to do some things that, actually, we're too tired to do. But as Faye Dunaway said when *Bonnie and Clyde* came out—she said she tried to get people what they wanted. That's a mistake, really. You can't do it. You use up everything you got when you give everybody what they want.

Let's see what we can do with this lovely, lovely thing that goes past all racial conflict and all kinds of conflicts. It is a reflective tune.

Sometime in your life you will have occasion to say, "What is this thing called time?" You know, what is *that*, the clock? You go to work by the clock, you get your martini in the afternoon by the clock and your coffee by the clock, and you have to get on the plane at a certain time, and arrive at a certain time. It goes on and on and on. Time is a dictator, as we know it. Where does it go? What does it do? Most of all, is it alive? Is it a thing that we cannot touch and is it alive? And then, one day, you look in the mirror—you're old—and you say, "Where did the time go?" We'll leave you with that one.

Nina Simone, introduction to her concert performance of "Who Knows Where the Time Goes" by Sandy Denny at Philharmonic Hall, New York, October 26, 1969.

How Forever Works
C. L. O'Dell

The soft tick of snow
landing in its own body —
what was left of time.

It then took every voice
to the ground with it.
In a way it listened to me
but also took me down.

However the world
remembered us,
it did so quietly, inside
a dying memory. Love me

anyway.

Artwork

Joseph-Antoine d'Ornano
Untitled, Cover artwork (2019)
Ink and watercolor
6 x 5 inches

4   Andy Russell
Dreaming of Africa (2017)
Acrylic on canvas
20 x 24 inches

14   Ferdinand Hodler
Die Strasse nach Evordes (1890)
Oil on canvas
25 x 18 inches

60   Rachel Long
Dagmar (2019)
Ink on paper
13 x 9 inches

76   Constant Nieuwenhuys
The Crowd II, detail (1996)
Oil on linen
64 x 67 inches

88   Constant Nieuwenhuys
Danseuse (1994)
Watercolor
Size Unknown

128   Caspar David Friedrich
Der Mönch am Meer (1808–1810)
Oil on canvas
43 x 68 inches

148   Gudrun Sallaberger-Plakolb
Shy (2015)
Pastel on paper
13 x 9 inches

172   Giorgio Morandi
Natura morta (1946)
Oil on canvas
15 x 18 inches

178   Vilhelm Hammershøi
Interior with a Young Man Reading (1898)
Oil on canvas
25 x 20 inches

198   Daniel Bodner
Truro Pines (2011)
Oil on linen
25 x 20 inches

210   Catherine Gareau-Blanchard
Birds of Spring (2019)
Watercolor
9 x 6 inches

Contributors

EDITORS

Jonathan Simons, Analog Sea's founding editor, is an American writer living in Germany.

Janos Tedeschi is a Swiss-Italian filmmaker and artist.

WRITERS

Libero Andreotti is an architect, critic, and historian living in Atlanta, Georgia.

James Baldwin (1924–1987) was an American writer and activist.

Sergio Benvenuto is an Italian psychoanalyst, philosopher, and writer.

Robert Bly is an American poet, essayist, and translator.

Ray Bradbury (1920–2012) was an American writer.

Pema Chödrön is an American Buddhist teacher and author.

Frédéric Chopin (1810–1849) was a Polish composer and pianist who lived much of his life in Paris.

Leonard Cohen (1934–2016) was a Canadian singer-songwriter and writer.

Guy Debord (1931–1994) was a French writer, philosopher, and founding member of the Situationist International.

Russell Edson (1935–2014) was an American poet, novelist, and artist.

Albert Einstein (1879–1955) was a German-born physicist who lived most of his life in Switzerland and the United States.

E. M. Forster (1879–1970) was a British essayist and novelist.

Pope Francis, born Jorge Mario Bergoglio, in Buenos Aires, Argentina, is the 266th pope and the first from the Americas.

Robert Frank is a Swiss-American photographer and filmmaker.

Kevin Fox Gotham is a professor of sociology at Tulane University in New Orleans.

Byung-Chul Han is a South Korean-born German author and philosopher based in Berlin.

Yuval Noah Harari is a historian and philosopher at the Hebrew University of Jerusalem.

Hermann Hesse (1877–1962) was a German poet, novelist, and painter.

Penelope Hewlett is a poet living in Worcestershire, United Kingdom.

Matthew Hollis is an editor and poet living in London.

Robert Irwin is an American abstract expressionist painter and installation artist.

Alejandro Jodorowsky is a Chilean-French filmmaker and author.

Fenton Johnson writes from Kentucky, Northern California, and southern Arizona.

Trebbe Johnson is an author and activist who lives in rural Pennsylvania.

Donald Kuspit is an American art critic, poet, and philosopher.

James Lasdun is a British writer living in the United States.

Don L. Lind is a retired American scientist and NASA astronaut.

Geert Lovink is a Dutch author, media theorist, and Internet critic.

Antonio Machado (1875–1939) was a Spanish poet from Seville.

Jerry Mander is an American author and founder of the International Forum on Globalization.

Mary Mercier is a poet living in Wisconsin.

Thomas Merton (1915–1968) was an American Trappist monk, activist, and writer.

Stephen Metcalf is a journalist based in New York.

C. L. O'Dell is a poet living in New York.

William Oxley is a poet living in England.

Geoff Pevere is a Canadian author and media critic.

Red Pine is a translator of Chinese texts and lives in Washington.

Oliver Sacks (1933–2015) was a British neurologist and author who lived most of his life in New York.

Carl Sandburg (1878–1967) was an American writer of poetry and prose.

Lesley Saunders is a poet living in the United Kingdom.

Robert Schumann (1810–1856) was a German composer, pianist, and music critic of the Romantic era.

Will Self is a British author and journalist.

Nina Simone (1933–2003) was an American singer and civil-rights activist.

Henry David Thoreau (1817–1862) was an American essayist, poet, and philosopher.

Sherry Turkle is a professor of sociology at MIT in Cambridge, Massachusetts.

Peter Valente is a writer and translator living in North Carolina.

Edmund de Waal is a porcelain artist and writer.

David Foster Wallace (1962–2008) was an American writer.

McKenzie Wark is an Australian-born writer and scholar based in New York.

Alan Watts (1915–1973) was a British-American philosopher.

Lin Yutang (1895–1976) was a Chinese philosopher and translator who lived much of his life in the United States.

INTERVIEWEES

Andreas Buchleitner is a professor of theoretical physics at the University of Freiburg, Germany.

Peter Mettler is a Canadian filmmaker and writer living between Toronto and the Swiss Alps.

ARTISTS

Daniel Bodner is an American painter dividing his time between Amsterdam, New York, and Massachusetts.

Joseph-Antoine d'Ornano is a Parisian painter and writer.

Caspar David Friedrich (1774–1840) was a German Romantic painter and printmaker.

Catherine Gareau-Blanchard is a mental-health professional and painter living in Montreal.

Vilhelm Hammershøi (1864–1916) was a Danish painter.

Ferdinand Hodler (1853–1918) was a Swiss painter.

Rachel Long is an American artist living in Southern Germany.

Giorgio Morandi (1890–1964) was an Italian still-life painter.

Constant Nieuwenhuys (1920–2005) was a Dutch painter, sculptor, graphic artist, author, and musician.

Andy Russell is a painter living in Andalucía, Spain.

Gudrun Sallaberger-Plakolb is an Austrian visual artist living in Basel, Switzerland.

Acknowledgments

5   "On Dreams" by Lin Yutang from *The Importance of Living.* Copyright © 1937, 1965 by Lin Tai-yi and Hsiang Ju Lan. Excerpt reprinted by permission of HarperCollins Publishers.

10   "Untitled" by Antonio Machado from *Times Alone: Selected Poems of Antonio Machado,* trans. Robert Bly. Translation © 1983 by Robert Bly. Reprinted by permission of Wesleyan University Press.

11   "Introduction" by Robert Bly from *Times Alone: Selected Poems of Antonio Machado.* Copyright © 1983 by Robert Bly. Excerpt reprinted by permission of Wesleyan University Press.

14   *Die Strasse nach Evordes* (1890) by Ferdinand Hodler (1853–1918). Copyright © 1931 by SIK-ISEA Zurich (Philipp Hitz). Kunst Museum Winterthur, Stiftung Oskar Reinhart.

15   "Peter Mettler: The Pursuit of Wonder" by Geoff Pevere, first published in *Take One Magazine* (September–November 2004). Copyright © 2004 by Geoff Pevere. Excerpt reprinted by permission of the publisher.

39   Interview with Don L. Lind, 1985, video © 1985 NASA Biographical Data, Lyndon B. Johnson Space Center, Houston, Texas.

61   "Life Continues" by Oliver Sacks from *Everything in its Place.* Copyright © 2019 by the Oliver Sacks Foundation. Reprinted by permission of Penguin Random House LLC.

70   "The Globalization of the Technocratic Paradigm" from *Laudato Si.* Copyright © 2015 by Libreria Editrice Vaticana. Excerpt reprinted by permission of Libreria Editrice Vaticana.

76   *The Crowd II* (1996) by Constant (1920–2005). Copyright © 2019 by Artists Rights Society (ARS), New York, c/o Pictoright Amsterdam. Digital image © 2019 by Constant and Fondation Constant. Collection Fondation Constant, NL (Tom Haartsen) c/o ARS, New York. Reprinted by permission of Fondation Constant and Artists Rights Society.

77   "Prologue" by Carl Sandburg from *Family of Man.* Copyright © 1955, 2015 by Museum of Modern Art, New York. Excerpt reprinted by permission of the museum.

82   "Objects of Desire" by Sherry Turkle from *What Should We Be Worried About?: Real Scenarios That Keep Scientists Up at Night,* ed. John Brockman. Copyright © 2014 by Edge Foundation, Inc. Reprinted by permission of HarperCollins Publishers.